Halfway Home

A Lesbian Romance

Anna Cove

For you.

Halfway Home

Chapter 1

SAVANNAH

"What are we waiting for, the apocalypse?"

My mother would roll in her grave if she were here to witness this. And if she were dead. Lori even grated on *me* as she chomped a piece of gum to expel her shattered nerves in the middle of a fancy restaurant. I suppressed the urge to reach under the table and touch her bouncing knee. You didn't see me bouncing around. Though I had enough energy that night to power a small town with a bicycle, I had the decency to keep still.

"People are more likely to do as you ask after a few drinks," I said, deliberately slowing my voice. "Can you settle down? Have a sip of your drink."

Lori let out an exasperated sigh and stilled, dropping her head. "I'm sorry. I'm so nervous."

I snaked my hand over the white cloth of our high-top table and gave her limp hand a squeeze. "You'll be fine. You don't have to do anything but what we discussed."

"Why can't Tim play wing man tonight?" Her tone prickled the hairs on the back of my neck. Though Lori *looked* like the thirty-year-old woman she was, with her sensible bob and pressed suit, she hadn't quite made it past seventeen in her social abilities.

"Because he has to nail down Senator Han

tonight, remember?"

Lori's bouncing and chewing doubled in pace. She glanced down in her lap, probably looking at her phone.

I took my hand away and folded it with the other one, regarding her. Lori and I lived and worked together, but we had less in common than a jack hammer and an ant. Her features—her soft, pink lips, her sandy brown eyes—were familiar to me, but her brain was so foreign. I was all contained energy, like a jaguar, while she was a skittish rabbit.

I checked my watch. "Quarter past nine. Are you ready?"

"No, I'm not ready," she said, slipping her phone in her pocket.

"Go to the bar." I stood, smoothing out my dress and touching the string of pearls on my neck. "Have another drink, and in twenty minutes, come tap me on the shoulder and whisper something to me."

"What should I say?" Lori tucked her waves behind her ear. She wasn't used to having the short hair and it fell forward, grazing her chin. She folded her arms and tapped her foot.

We'd already talked about this, but I went over it again. "Whisper some sweet nothings, darling. Anything. It doesn't matter."

Lori's big eyes went wider. "You know what? I bet you can do it alone. You don't need me."

"You'll be fine," I said, rubbing her shoulder. It was the most contact we'd had in months and my hand tingled with it.

"I won't. I'll wreck it all."

I resisted glancing behind me. Lori's voice was

rising, and if she didn't stop she would blow my cover.

If she hadn't already.

I had to stop this.

I grabbed her shoulders, steadying her in place. "I'm not going to lie to you. This is huge for us. A win—getting this one vote—could get us the promotion we've been hoping for."

"A promotion for *you,* maybe. You're the superstar."

"We're a team. Right now, I need you to do this little thing for me, okay? All you have to do is show up and I'll do the rest."

I bent at the knees, seeking out Lori's eyes. She eked out a nod. Then I turned her around and gave her a little push toward the bar. "Twenty minutes, okay?"

"Okay, okay," she said. Her phone came out a moment later. Head bent, she made her way into the lounge. I prayed she wouldn't come out with a piece of gum in her hair and the phone attached to her forehead. There was still a part of the south embedded in me that missed common decency.

As I strolled through the softly lit dining area, the famous faces of D.C. smiled back from their frames on the wall. A hall of accomplishment, of power. The famous faces of now, the live faces, barely paid me attention. High powered politicians leaning far too close to smiling interns. A clerk whose hand was on the knee of a woman who definitely wasn't his wife. A group of female staffers, dressed in suits and fashionable jewelry, toasting a win.

This was *my* crowd. I knew them like they were

my own family, better than my own family. They didn't know me yet, but soon they would. Not the tourists, or outsiders, but the insiders. The people on these hallowed walls.

Nestled in the corner was my target, sitting with a companion. He wore a pressed white shirt, a bolo, and a broad gap-toothed smile. The spirits showed in his rosy cheeks, watery eyes, and the ice clinking against the sides of the near-empty crystal glass in his hand.

Near-empty worked in my favor.

As I passed a young waiter, I gave him my best smile. His face turned crimson under my stare, and he tripped over his own feet. My hands went to steady him, but that only made him shake like a leaf in a hurricane. I slipped away with apologies, more smiles, and a plate of half a dozen oysters.

Never arrive to a dinner party empty-handed.

As I walked past the table with the senator and his wife, I looked over my shoulder and caught the senator's wife's eye. Stopping short, I turned on my heel.

"Heavens to Betsy," I said, turning on my southern accent, "that necklace is absolutely divine. Tell me, where did you get it?"

A patchwork of red blotches webbed the woman's neck and jaw.

"I was just passing by and your gem just stopped me dead. What is it? Sapphire? Do you mind if I… look more closely?"

The woman's fingers moved from loosely clasping her necklace to the napkin in her lap. She lifted her chin, recovering her poise. "Not at all, dear.

Go right ahead."

I leaned forward, picking up the sapphire gem resting on her sternum. It sparkled in the overhead light. "Did this fine gentleman buy it for you?"

The woman chuckled. "Nope. I bought it myself."

"Even better." Easing the pendant back down, I let my fingers brush against her neck. It wasn't a sexual move, not at all, but I'd come to find many women craved these little intimate touches, especially when they were married to attention-grubbing narcissists.

So far, I hadn't paid this particular narcissist any attention, though he *was* my target. Sometimes, a glancing blow, more than a direct hit, decimated.

I straightened, my back to him. "I'm sorry, I'm being rude. My name is Savannah Burns," I said, my hand outstretched to Mrs. Drummond.

"Caroline Drummond."

I gave her a firm handshake, just like I was taught, and turned to Senator Drummond to do the same.

As soon as it was appropriate without being rude, I turned back to Mrs. Drummond. "I was about to tuck in to my oysters at the bar when a particularly rowdy group of staffers got a little too friendly. I welcome company as much as the next lady, but these guys were free with their words and hands, if you know what I mean. I wanted to see if there was any room to eat in here, but…"

I let my glance ride over the gathered crowd. Thankfully, there wasn't an empty table in the group.

"You must join us," Mrs. Drummond said.

"Caroline," the Senator said under his breath,

just loud enough so I could hear.

"Oh, don't be rude, Len, let the girl sit. Be my guest. Come, sit next to me."

"Oh no, I couldn't possibly horn in on your romantic dinner."

Caroline, having found her voice somewhere along the way, let out a delicate laugh. "We haven't had a romantic dinner since 1987. Sit, I insist. It'll be nice to have some young blood around."

"In that case, care for some oysters?" I slid into the space left by Caroline, placing my plate on the table between us. It was a small booth, and our arms pressed against one another. Caroline sat ramrod straight, which, if I wasn't wrong, she hadn't been doing when I arrived. A light rose perfume and an open energy radiated off of her.

Which is more than I could say for the senator sitting across from me, whose smile had turned into a scowl as he stared into his empty glass. He waved over a waiter and ordered another drink and dessert. I ordered a glass of wine. Once we were all settled, Caroline turned to me.

"It's terribly rude of me to ask—"

"You can ask me anything. I am an open book." An open book ready to close the book on landmark environmental legislation for this century. If only I could get the vote of this stubborn man sitting across from me drinking his thirty-year-old scotch.

"Are you in your mid-twenties or so?"

"Thirty-one a couple weeks ago, but thank you for the compliment." I winked at her, then fingered my glass of Chardonnay.

"And what made you move up north?"

"I wanted to experience a different way of living, so I moved to Massachusetts for college. I tried to go back home afterward, but I only made it halfway."

"To this place?"

"I really do love working here." I shrugged, letting my shoulders fall. Like the polite woman she was, Caroline Drummond was making the conversation all about me, but I needed to turn it around. I had a schedule. "To think, I wouldn't have found such fine company for dinner tonight if I hadn't stopped."

"Cheers to that." Mrs. Drummond raised her glass, and we clinked them together.

I took a sip of my wine, letting my lashes fall over my eyes, then I straightened. "Call me a fool, but I'm just realizing… are you *Senator* Drummond? From Florida?" Before he could answer, I turned my body to Caroline. "And you're *Caroline* Drummond. Oh, my stars and garters, I can't believe I didn't make the connection before. You're involved with that organization for the homeless—"

"The Coalition for Dignity for the Homeless. Yes."

"I read about you in the Post. You're creating those beautiful quilts. My mother tried to teach me how to sew when I was little, but I poked more holes in my fingers than the fabric and she eventually let me out of it. I was a bit of a wild child, I must admit."

The woman laughed again. "My daughter was, too, Lord Almighty. But seeing you here gives me hope."

"You are too much, Mrs. Drummond."

"Call me, Caroline, please," she said, her

cheekbones pinking.

"Caroline, then. I found this gorgeous fabric store, and I'd love to donate some squares to your organization."

We exchanged information. All through this conversation and card switching, Senator Drummond watched me over the rim of his glass. He had good reason to be wary, he just didn't know why yet, but like any good politician he could smell blood in the water.

"Tell me," I said, turning once again to his wife. "How did you get involved with the homeless?"

Caroline Drummond told me a touching story of how she'd walked down the streets of Tallahassee on a cold night and saw a man shivering under a tattered, dirty blanket, and gave him her fur coat. It sparked an idea that turned into a nationwide organization.

Like tunnels lining up, I could see a straight shot to where I needed to go from where I was. I had to time this part perfectly with Lori's entrance. I checked my watch. Five more minutes. Could I do it? Of course I could. I was Savannah Burns.

"Florida has endured terrible hurricanes lately," I said. "You must see your homeless population skyrocketing."

"Oh yes, and it becomes even more of a problem during storms."

"Do y'all have a plan? According to scientists, these big weather events are only going to happen more often now."

Mrs. Drummond's eyes flicked to her husband for the first time in a while. In her eyes, I saw an *I told you so* and a stubborn determination to do the right thing.

"I see what you're doing," Senator Drummond said. He leaned toward his wife. "I knew her name was familiar. Ms. Burns is a lobbyist for the environmental legislation up for a vote tomorrow. She's been using you, darling."

Mrs. Drummond pulled upright in that imperial manner women of a certain age in the south have. I couldn't read her gaze until it moved back to her husband. A flash of mischief twitched in the muscles beside her eye. "She's right, though."

The senator's nostrils flared. I pushed down a smile. *Way to go, Caroline.*

I kept my focus on her. She was the way in. "Florida is impacted more than any other state in the country. You have more destructive hurricanes each year and no defense for it. This legislation will halt the rapid temperature climb—"

The senator pounded his fists on the table. "Bullshit. You don't know that."

I wasn't going to back down from a little bluster. "What do we ever know? This is all new territory. All we can do is try."

"And what about the oranges?" Mrs. Drummond asked.

I thought the senator would blow the few gray strands of hair he had left straight into the air, he was so mad. His face turned beet red. His blue eyes grew watery. "What about the damned oranges?" he said through gritted teeth.

"They're blighted. They're falling off the trees." Caroline kept her perfect poise even though her neck was growing red.

"Since when did you take an interest in science, my dear wife?"

"I've always been interested if you would just give me the time of day."

Oo. This was quickly disintegrating, and it didn't bode well for me. I had to bring it back around. I had two more minutes. Like most of Washington, Drummond had a few ink stains on his record, and I knew about them. It was my job, but I wasn't going to pull them out unless I had to. "If you're worried about the politics of this, I can smooth it over."

"My party would skewer me." He said, fully facing me. "Absolutely not."

"I can help you spin this. It's good for Florida. It would get you the undecided vote. It's a bipartisan deal, and it includes market-based incentives that respect private property owners. You can do this. You can be the senator at the forefront of climate change."

He shook his head and crossed his arms. Other lobbyists may have had some backroom deal to give him, but I didn't have that. That's not how I worked. I did have knowledge. I did know *people*. They were my thing. Speaking of people… where was Lori?

"Do you remember why you got into politics?" Caroline asked, surprising me and her husband by the look of his face.

"Caroline," he said.

"Because you wanted to do good."

"That's enough," he hissed.

Come on, Lori. Come on. I may want his vote, but I didn't want Caroline to get the brunt of this.

Lori emerged from around the corner, shaking her head at some invisible voice.

Oh, *Lord*, help me. Why had I asked her to help? I knew she couldn't do it. I tried to send her one of my winning smiles. She stopped, blinked, and turned around.

Wait.

It was too late. I could either run after her, or do this myself. I didn't like what that meant, but I didn't have a chance. If I blew it here, I would blow my chances to impress my boss, Tim. It would show him I couldn't handle the pressure. That was unacceptable.

I sent a calming breath and a sip of wine to my speeding heart. "I'm sorry, Senator Drummond, it's so rude of me to talk politics at dinner. Let's drop it. Please accept my apologies."

"No need to apologize, dear," Caroline said, slipping her hand over mine. She gave me a squeeze with her bony fingers and smiled lightly at me, sending a piercing gaze toward her husband.

"I think we have a friend in common. Do you know someone named Stevens?" I asked.

It was a tiny, almost imperceptible freezing, but I caught it. A slight widening of the eyes in Senator Drummond.

"A Stevens."

"Umm…" I said, tapping my chin with my finger. "Yes, Stevens."

I unabashedly kept my eyes on the Senator now. He wiped his brow, looking a little peaked if you asked me. "Senator? Do you know the aide I'm talking about? Tall? Dark?" *Stunningly beautiful and not your wife.*

Plan B had a sharp edge to it, but a project always needed the right tools, and the right tool for this was a knife.

"No, I don't know anyone by the name Stevens. I'm sorry," Senator Drummond said, collecting himself.

"Oh, that's too bad. She's a friend of mine. We're very close and—"

Senator Drummond's hand shot out. His grip burned against my wrist as he pulled me toward him. The table slammed into the tops of my legs.

"Leonard," Caroline shouted.

Senator Drummond's face was so close to mine I could smell the scotch on his breath, could see the purpled spider veins and pores on his nose. "Vote yes," I mouthed.

A threat. A knife to the balls.

Blood pumped through my ears along with adrenaline, and I didn't hear Caroline's screams until he had let go. I dropped back into the bench. Caroline fussed over me, but I kept eye contact with *him*. He had to know I was serious, and he still didn't give me an answer.

I turned to Caroline. "I'm sorry I've destroyed your dinner," I said again. "I have something to tell you."

"You know what, Caroline?"

Senator Drummond's voice was so changed, we both turned to him. "I think you have a point about the oranges. Maybe I should reconsider this before the vote tomorrow."

"Excellent." Knife retracted. I smiled, smoothed

my dress, and backed out of the booth. "I know when I'm not welcome any longer. It was lovely to meet you, Caroline. Senator Drummond. I'll be in contact."

"Please, do," Caroline said, missing the double meaning of the conversation. Or, at least, pretending to miss it.

I took my leave, my heart racing with success—*success*. Of course, nothing was official yet, but it would be tomorrow. It would all come together. I was sure of it. As I made my way back through the Hall of Political Fame and through the bar, someone caught my arm. Lori.

"I'm sorry," she said. "I couldn't do it."

"I get it," I said, but I didn't. I didn't understand how she couldn't do one simple thing. How she couldn't push through whatever fears plagued her, for me. For us. For our success. Just being in her presence was bringing me down from my high.

"Do you want to go home and celebrate?" she asked.

"Actually, I'm going to tie up a few loose ends at work," I said, feeling the weight come into my shoes after my glorious flight.

"Are you sure?"

"Yeah."

"Can I walk you to the building?"

Suddenly, I couldn't stay one more moment in her presence. "You go on ahead. I need the ladies' room."

Lori's smile faltered. As we split, the excitement started to return. I'd won. I'd won. After all this time and hard work, victory was mine. I could see now why people stayed in D.C. The game was seductive.

Chapter 2

CASEY

"Stop! Wait!"

I soared past the tuxedoed host at his podium, around a table, and along the bar, scouring the walls for a bathroom sign. At a couple blocking my way, I bent low, clasping my knees. "Excuse me," I called, bombing through them in a rolling cannonball.

Some scoffed, others—a few—smiled. With my pink-tinged hair and my bright blue skates, I seemed to draw from both ends of the spectrum. Smiles or judgment. I wasn't surprised in an old school building like this, located so close to the Capitol, to get more of the latter. I stood and skated around a corner, leaving the host in my wake. Up ahead, a sign marking the women's restroom appeared.

I let out a breath. "Finally."

I skated toward it with all my strength, my wheels gliding over the thin carpet, and hooked around the corner of the doorway through the swinging door. The door stopped, slamming against something solid. The something solid grunted.

"Are you hurt?" I called, cringing, half because I felt bad and half because I really needed to pee.

"I didn't need that nose, anyway."

"Are you away from the door now?"

"Wait—" she said, but I was already opening the

door. The woman in question had her round ass in the air. She wore an expensive-looking blood orange dress and held a jacket in her hands. She was picking something up off the floor. Pills, it looked like.

"Jesus, I'm so sorry." I knelt and helped her gather the pills into her little Altoids container. She closed it and slipped it in her pocket and stood, avoiding my gaze. A blot of blood dripped down her nose as she blinked at me.

"You're bleeding."

"Yeah, well, you're dangerous on those things." Touching her nose, she tilted her chin at my skates.

I crossed to the counter and ended in a half-circle, pulling down the paper towels, thick as cloth. This bathroom was fancy. It smelled of rose petals—real rose petals—though I couldn't see any on the perfectly clean and dry counters. The sinks had some of those faucets that looked like mini well spouts and cushioned benches along the wall for waiting patrons. I slid to the woman and handed her the towels.

"Thanks," she said.

"It's the least I could do." I was still out of breath from sprinting down the hall, and now there was a chance the host would come in here, perhaps with security. And I still had to pee. Badly. But there was this beautiful woman staring at me and she had slate-gray eyes and there was something about blondes with odd eye colors I couldn't resist and—holy shit—I needed to pee.

"Stay there," I said, breaking away. I whipped around the corner and skated into the stall, closed the door behind me, and did my thing. Only when I finished did I notice that this fancy, perfectly clean bathroom had precisely zero toilet paper left in this stall.

"Are you still there?" I asked.

"I wouldn't dare disobey your orders," the pretty woman said.

Wow, she was sassy. I liked it. My heart sang in tune with my smiling mouth. "Mind slipping me some toilet paper?"

The woman's heels clicked against the tiled floor, tracing a path into the stall next to me. A sensibly manicured hand offered me a roll of toilet paper. My chipped fingernails looked like a nervous sixth grader's next to hers as I took the roll. "Thanks," I said, unraveling the paper. "What brings you here?"

"To the bathroom?"

"Sure, why not," I said.

She paused, and I stopped moving, stopped breathing, to listen for a clue to what she was doing. Was she grinning? Or was she rolling her eyes, ready to flee from my irritating presence as soon as she could.

"I'm celebrating, actually."

I practically choked on my badly needed intake of breath. "In the bathroom?"

"Why not? It's a perfectly lovely bathroom."

The pretty girl had a sense of humor. This was getting more and more interesting by the minute. I flushed the toilet and maneuvered out of the stall. "The loveliest of them all," I said, in my best witchy voice.

Smack. Ping-pong ball in your court, honey.

She laughed, a low throaty chuckle that only

added depth to the image I had crafted of her. As she did, she reached the sinks, threw away her bloody tissue, and leaned a hip up against the counter, tipping her head, exposing a long expanse of bare neck. A pretty girl with a sense of humor. My kryptonite.

Just like that, the ball was back on my side of the table.

"What are you celebrating?" I asked, turning off the water and reaching toward the paper towel dispenser, pointedly *not* looking at her.

I still noticed her staring at my exposed navel, though. The question was, was she appreciating it? Or judging me for it? The pink circles in her cheeks implied the former.

"You would probably find it boring," she said.

"What makes you say that?"

"Look at you." She gestured toward me. "You're a total badass. Blue skates. Pink hair. You wear a belly shirt and little shorts and… Oh, sweet baby Jesus, what is wrong with me? Must be the wine."

She covered her eyes, but not before I saw her gaze turn. Not before her lids lowered and her lips parted and… did I see her eyes dilate? Was I just imagining that? I finished drying my hands and threw the paper towel in the trash. *Slam. Dunk.*

I folded my arms. "Go on. I'm enjoying myself."

She pulled her hands away, a smile playing on her lips. "You're just fishing for compliments now."

"What if I was?"

"I would tell you to get a bigger rod because you're about to rope a whale."

Cracks developed in my body, cracks that let the

heat seep into my veins and over my heart and up my chest and throat. Cracks that threatened to turn into a volcanic eruption if she wasn't careful where she stepped.

I decided to back up, to figure out where we were in this whole thing. "How are you celebrating? Other than wine?"

The woman sighed, leaning against the stalls. For the first time she looked tired. Worn out. "Time alone before I go to work, I suppose."

"Tonight?"

"Yeah."

"How about a party instead? With me?"

"A party?"

"Yes, you know, those things with drinks and music and people."

Outside the door, the static fuzz of a walkie-talkie came closer. "Do me a favor?" I asked, shooting my fingers to her to lips stop her from answering.

The woman blinked. I released my fingers, though the soft silk of her skin lingered there.

"What's in it for me?" The side of her mouth twitched.

"Chocolate? More wine? My undying gratitude? My everlasting soul?"

"Sold."

I couldn't help but smile as I placed my hands on her shoulders, cementing the deal. "Cover for me with security? Tell them you're alone."

The woman's eyebrow flicked up.

"Are you uncomfortable with that?"

"No. Go to the stall," she said, pushing my arms

off her shoulders.

"Now look who's barking out orders," I said, happily going along. I skated to the closest stall and perched on the pristine toilet, pulling my feet up just in case.

"Excuse me ma'am," I heard a moment later. "Have you seen a woman with pink hair and roller skates in there?"

"Nope," the woman said.

A smile stretched the skin on my face as a snicker caught in my chest. Something else bloomed there, too. A warmth.

"Are you certain? She came through here and there's nowhere else to go."

"Don't you think I'd notice a woman with pink hair on roller skates? I'm not blind."

She said it with so much disdain, I had to cover my mouth to keep the laugh from spilling like a bucket of marbles on a seesaw.

"Do you mind if I just have a look around—"

"Didn't your mama raise you better than that? The ladies' room? Of course I mind. You don't want me to tell management you're scaring people away from the restaurant, do you? I mean, if you go snooping around in here I can tell you I won't be coming here ever again. Trust me, you do not want to get on my bad side."

"Of course. I'm sorry, Ms. Burns," the man said, a slight tremble in his voice.

I'd only known this Ms. Burns a few minutes, but I already knew I didn't want to get on her bad side. In fact, the more she spoke, the more I wanted to get on her good side. As soon as I heard the door close, I let my feet down and glided over the tiny bumpy tiles until I was a foot away from her. She had her hand near her mouth and shook her head.

"That was *amazing*," I said. "Please teach me your ways, master."

"Oh, stop it," Savannah rolled her eyes and flicked her hand in a valley girl exaggeration. "That was a lot of fun, though."

"Sounded like it. I almost came out to join in the fun."

"Good thing you didn't. You would have made me a liar."

"How am I ever going to repay you?" I asked, my voice dropping half an octave of its own damn accord.

"Your soul, remember?"

This close to her, my feelings about her good sides were only growing stronger. She had a lot of good sides. Dimples, for one. I was a sucker for dimples. She was tall, almost as tall as I was on my skates, and obviously spent some time on her appearance, enough to show she cared but not enough to imply obsession. She had two beauty marks, one under her left eye and the other at the corner of her lip. I couldn't stop tracing the line between them.

And I wasn't misreading it now. She was sending me all the signs. Echoing my posture, leaning toward me.

"And how you would you like to claim your prize?" I asked, my voice raspy as a soul singer's.

"What if…?" Our eyes locked, neither of us looking away. My heart beat so loud it was like it had set up a speaker system in my head. She didn't have to finish her sentence. All she had to do was lean forward, crossing into my personal space.

The moment our lips touched fear fled, chased out by pure lust. The woman held my face like she cared about me, a little moan escaping from her lips. The sound kicked up the volume in my ears and in my center. I pressed my body against hers, and her soft curves melted into me.

Her tongue snaked its way into my mouth, and in that moment I didn't care who she was. I wouldn't have cared if she was a witch who could *really* steal my soul, I would have given it to her. I melted into her, and then she pulled away.

Her body first. Her mouth next. Her gaze last. She leaned over the sink, out of breath, her shoulders up to her ears.

I said nothing, pressing a hand to my heartbeat to see if it would calm.

"Thank you," she said.

Was that a thing that people did? Thank one another for kisses? "No… problem?"

"I better go."

"Wait," I said, catching her hand. Her fingers tightened over mine, giving me the courage to say what I had to say next. "What about the party?"

"You've given me all the party I need." A soft smile dawned on her face as she gave me a squeeze and let go.

When she dropped my hand, it was like Jack Frost had blown a gust of wind my way. There'd be other women, of course, but when would be the next time I could find someone like her? With a connection like this? My body dictated the terms. It wanted more time. It wanted more of her. It wanted *more*.

I skated to my backpack and pulled a purple Crayola marker from the outside pocket, then I crossed to the woman and tugged her arm toward me.

"This is my number," I said, writing on her pale skin, "and this is the address of the party. Text me if you're coming and I'll be sure to wait for you there."

The woman blinked at my fingers touching her. I looked so… mangy… next to her, dirty almost.

"Thanks," she said again, slipped out of my grasp, and disappeared like a ghost.

The only thing that reminded me she was real was the sweet taste of her lingering on my lips.

Chapter 3

SAVANNAH

What is going on with me?

Less than an hour after my bathroom run-in, I gripped the edge of my wood veneer desk, staring at the Impressionist prints on the wall. Time seemed to slow and speed at once. My brain raced but my body wouldn't go with it. Most of the work for the vote the next day was done. Not even I could find enough work to fill the next hours.

That kiss certainly hadn't helped. What had possessed me to do that? It had been a whirlwind moment, a one-time thing. There was no other way to think about it, at this point. I had Lori and my job, and I couldn't go around kissing random women. Especially if it left me feeling like both the tortoise and the hare in the race.

The words on the piece of paper in front of me dimmed. The only light in the tiny work office I shared with Lori was an antique banker's lamp on my desk. Overhead lights gave me migraines, and the steakhouse had done enough damage on that front. I tried to focus one more time, but it was no good.

Sweet Baby Jesus, I'd kissed a random woman. She wasn't even my type. Way too funky and free-spirited. She probably slept under the stars for fun.

I pulled up my sleeve, her number present and

real and sharp on my wrist. When was the last time someone had written something on my arm? Sixth grade maybe? That time, it was Jen Peters, and she'd drawn a heart on my arm and I'd blushed so hard I had to run away straight after. I'd come a long way since her, except—I dropped my face in my hands— I'd run away from the pink-haired woman, too. A sharp laugh escaped my lips at the thought.

This time I had a reason. Lori. My job. I'd crafted a stable life here, one I would have dreamed of as a kid, and I didn't need to blow it up. It had been just a kiss. No need for social suicide.

I licked my fingers and rubbed at the phone number on my arm. The numbers smudged together, creating a purpled mess that looked like a bruise. I scrubbed harder, reddening the skin around and under the numbers. I scrubbed and scrubbed until the numbers were illegible. Then I let my sleeve fall over my arm.

Erasing the number did nothing to erase the woman on my lips, her fingers on my pulse. The ease with which her body melted into mine. The quickening of my heartbeat as I remembered those moments. I let out a breath, trying to blow out some of the pulsing heat. When was the last time Lori and I had touched like that? Or touched at all? Going home to her tonight after that… could I do it?

It could go one of two ways. I would slip into bed and she wouldn't even wake up. Or I would slip into bed and keep thinking of this woman with the pink hair and be unable to stop myself from kissing Lori and quenching whatever this heat was in my stomach. She would know something was up. She would question me, ask me where all of this was coming from. What would I say? I'm hot for you because I met someone else? When in the world had that been a turn-on?

I picked at the edge of the sleeve on my left arm, still warm from all the rubbing. I couldn't go home. I couldn't stay here. Both would make me crazy. Going out wouldn't help.

It seemed as if I was barreling downhill on a bike and my brakes were out and I couldn't take any turns.

Oh, darn it.

Leaning over, I pulled up my sleeve and shoved my forearm under the antique lamp. The number was completely unrecognizable, but the address was still readable, to a certain extent. It was in the Shaw neighborhood in northwest D.C. I could take the green line or an Uber and be there in a few minutes. Pink had mentioned texting her to make sure she was still there, but that wasn't an option now. What if I just showed up? What was the worst that could happen?

She wouldn't be there and I would go home.

But I knew myself. If I never went at all, the questions would fill the spaces of my mind. It would become my obsession, the thing I couldn't leave well enough alone. I had to go. It was for the best, for everyone. I grabbed my clutch and keys from the desk and marched out the door.

One night of celebration. I deserved it.

...

I knew I didn't belong as soon as someone opened the door and stumbled outside. He had green hair gelled into a Mohawk and eyeliner thicker than mine. This someone took a moment to focus on me. "Do you have a cigarette?"

"No, sorry," I said.

He grunted, using the wall as a railing to move down the hall.

The wine bottle in my hand suddenly seemed naïve, quaint, though it wasn't a cheap bottle of wine. I had become so used to the conventional parties in the capital I'd forgotten to ask what kind of party this was. Thankfully, no one had seen me, except the guy with the Mohawk, but I wasn't sure he had even really seen me, so I turned around and walked away.

"You came," rang a familiar voice.

Sorry, wrong person, I almost said, but that was stupid. Pink had seen me and slinking away would mean making a scene, and I didn't need to make a scene. I smiled and turned around. But as I caught sight of her, my smile practically dropped off my face.

Pink was wearing the short shorts and the skates she had on earlier, but she had traded her relatively conservative cropped T-shirt for a crocheted top in the shape of a diamond pointing toward her belly button, as if she needed anything to draw attention there. Through the top part of the crochet pattern, on her chest, she had a heart tattooed. Not the silly playground kind of heart like Jen Peters had drawn on my wrist in sixth grade, but an anatomically correct heart. A heart so real-looking, I could almost imagine it beating.

I blinked the thought away and focused on her feet instead. "Do you ever take those off?"

Pink twirled, her hands up in the air. She stopped, her eyes glowing. "Rarely. Only when I need to escape and on special occasions."

She skated toward me, her face broadened in a wide smile. Her hair was in little pigtails and her eye makeup was heavier now, ready for a nighttime party. She circled me and slid her hand into mine like she'd done it a thousand times. "I'm so happy you're here," she said.

A warmth spread through me from her hand all the way to my heart and my groin. When had I last felt something? It made me want to… whoop? That was an odd thing to want, especially for me. I pushed the urge down where I wouldn't be able to find it any longer. I lifted the wine bottle. "I brought wine," I said, stupidly. "But maybe this isn't that kind of party?"

"It's perfect. How sweet of you." She was still holding my hand, and now she took the bottle of wine from me and skated slowly down the hall. I had to walk fast to keep pace, but somehow I didn't care.

She had so bewitched me I'd forgotten how utterly out-of-place I was until we entered the apartment. It was packed with hot and sweaty people dancing in the center of the room, couples making out or talking along the edges. Flashing lights like a nightclub. Pink pulled me straight through to the kitchen where a table was set up with punch and a plundered chip bowl. Only then did she let go of my hand. "Do you want some wine? Punch?"

"Do you live here?" I asked.

"God, no," she said, letting out a little laugh. "Denise, the woman who owns the apartment is in the other room. I'll have to introduce you to her at some point."

The red solo cup I picked up from the table brought back memories of my college party days. Those days were certainly gone. Even so, it felt right ladling a spoonful of the pink mystery punch into my cup. "I feel…" When was the last time I had said those words? I continued. "I feel silly here. I don't even know your name and I'm in a stranger's apartment. I've been calling you Pink in my head."

She leaned her hip against the table as she picked up a chip and crunched down on it. Of course she ate chips. She probably ate anything she wanted and magically maintained her incredible body. "That's my roller derby name. Pink Lightning."

"Roller derby. Ha. That's not surprising at all."

"See? I'm not a *total* stranger. You know something about me."

"It's not exactly rocket science. Everyone who meets you could guess you were probably into roller derby."

"What gives it away, the skates?"

I chuckled, hiding my mouth with my cup. This woman made me smile so often my jaw ached.

"Want to hear what I've been calling you?"

"Yeah, I do," I said, lowering the cup.

Her gaze flicked to my lips for a moment before returning to my eyes. "Sweet Lips."

I let my face drop into my hands and groaned. "I can't believe I kissed you earlier. That wasn't like me."

"I'm not complaining," she said, edging closer. "In fact, I'm hoping, since you're here, it'll happen again."

I lifted my face to see if she was serious. Did women flirt like this outside of male fantasies and books and movies? Apparently so, because though Pink Lightning seemed to do little without smiling, she wasn't smiling now.

I couldn't. I had to set a boundary. I was here for fun. "I can't," I choked out before I lost the ability to deny to her.

"Good thing you aren't *you* tonight. You're Sweet Lips."

Suddenly, my heart lodged in my throat. I lifted my cup of punch and gulped it down in one go, hoping the barrage of alcohol would push the vital organ down where it belonged. The alcohol burned. Strong. I cringed.

What could go wrong here? My whole life? But how was that going now, anyway? My life didn't even seem like mine. What if… what if I could pretend it wasn't? Just for one night? Maybe it would help me out of this exhaustion. So far, just being near this woman was doing wonders for that. What if I could let go? Just once?

The alcohol dimmed the bright overhead lights of the room enough to give me the courage I needed to take the next step. Just like when I was trying to convince Senator Drummond to go my way, I felt a surge of adrenaline, my heart beating strong. Life pulsing through my veins.

"I'd like that." I took Pink's hand and pulled her toward the quieter section of the apartment.

She skated, humming along to the music on the radio. I pulled her through a crowd of people speaking French and caught a wisp of a Scandinavian-accented voice. Sweet Lips. As her, I could relax. Sweet Lips didn't have a girlfriend at home or a job to return to tomorrow. The alcohol was starting to take hold, to turn down the volume on my steady stream of thoughts. I took another sip of the punch as we approached an open section of the couch.

I sat and Pink plopped down next to me.

"Tell me what you do," I asked. "For work."

"What a boring question."

I let out an astonished chuckle. Who was this woman who wouldn't even follow the most basic tenets of small talk? She would have been eaten alive by the women of my youth, whipped into shape *real* fast.

"Come on. Try harder. Ask me something else," she said.

My mind went blank. It never went blank. I was always a step ahead of everyone else around me, but Pink made me feel like I'd shown up to a French exam when I'd taken Spanish all year long.

She tucked her legs up under her like her skates were just her feet. "Oh, fine. I'll answer your question. I skate," she yelled over the music.

I shifted closer so I could ask my next question without yelling. "How do you make money?"

"I don't." She shrugged.

This did not compute. "Then how to do you live?"

"Mostly I crash on people's couches. I'm trying to skate all fifty states in a year, plus D.C., of course. Hence…"

"Why you're here."

"Yeah." She leaned forward, her breath tickling my ear. It sent shivers down the side of my neck, and I wondered if she could see my attraction to her in the little bumps there. She continued. "I'm raising money for an organization called Voices for Love that gives foster kids a bag of their own stuff and assigns them penals when they get placed into homes. I've already raised thousands of dollars in a few months."

"My God, that's amazing." I backed away to make eye contact, shaking my head at this bewildering woman. Why hadn't she started with that? Most people, even those inclined to philanthropy, would brag about their accomplishments to try to impress others. But the first thing Pink had done was ask me to help her escape from a restaurant bathroom. She'd started with that and here I was. Wouldn't I have just shut her down if she had asked any other way? Maybe I could learn something from her.

"What do you do for fun?" she asked. Her lips brushed my ear this time, sending a shiver straight through me.

Work? Negotiate? Pink wouldn't find that interesting. I was over-thinking this, all of it, which was so very Savannah. "Let's talk some more about you. You're much more interesting than me."

Pink looked from one of my eyes to the other. She had a freckle on the whites of one of her eyes. Another oddity. The heart on her chest was so close I could trace it with the pad of my finger. Because I wasn't exactly me in that moment, I raised my hand

and touched her on the aortic valve. It was as if I'd pressed the *go* button. She leaned forward and caught my lips with hers and I tensed.

No, my brain yelled.

Yes, my body said, a deep bass note of yes. With a groan, I melted into her. She pulled me closer. My tongue slipped past her lips and she leaned on me and I leaned back on someone else and her hand trailed up my leg and only then did I realize I was out of my depth. I pulled away, again. No sex. That's where I would draw the boundary line. No sex.

"Want to see pictures of the states I've done so far?" Pink asked, chipper as before, as if the kiss hadn't happened.

I managed a wobbly smile, forcing my breaths to come evenly. If Pink could fake it, so could I. "Sure. I'd love to."

She brought out a smartphone, which for some reason seemed analogous to who she was, and opened her Instagram account. She showed me videos of her grinding on curbs, swinging on trees, singing at the top of her lungs as she ate an ice cream cone and always—always—on her skates. Child-like fun and energy spilled through the screen and touched the tips of my fingers.

What am I doing here?

"How many followers do you have?" I couldn't help asking, though it came from the place of my work self, not so much from the hot lips self. Or was it sweet lips? Lord, my lips tingled just thinking of it.

"Oh, I don't know. A hundred thousand maybe?"

"A... what? You could be making quadruple that..." I drew in a breath and closed my eyes. *Stop it, Savannah. This is not work.* "Will you excuse me for a moment? I need to go to the ladies' room."

Pink blinked. "It's down the hall on the right."

I could feel her eyes on me as I walked away. I'd never been in the presence of anyone so brazen about their affections, about what they wanted. People were often conflicted, operating on complex layers in systems, changing with whoever they met. I had a feeling Pink never operated like that. Whatever she felt she put out there. How could she do that? She was so... fearless.

The bathroom was small and neat, but dingy in the way old bathrooms got after a while. Never really clean until the next renovation. I locked the door and leaned on the pedestal sink, staring in the mirror. A row of light lines marred my forehead. There were bags under my eyes. What did this woman see in me? Plain old me?

In my college days I would have been all over this party, dancing and drinking and singing and talking and enjoying myself. But I was so far from that time, the memory no longer seemed like mine. I smudged the circles under one eye like it was makeup I could rub away. I smoothed the wrinkles on my forehead. It had only been ten years since those college days, yet I felt used up. Old. Frumpy. Tired.

When do I have fun?

At work? But was that really *fun*? Was it enough?

I plucked open my clutch, found my little container of pick-me-ups, opened it, crushed a couple of them on the edge of the sink, and sent the line right up my nose. Almost immediately, the uptick of energy kicked in, the corners of my mouth pulled up in a smile.

There. There was the old Savannah. The fun Savannah. She'd just been hiding for far too long.

Chapter 4

CASEY

Lips was too tense, which meant I wasn't doing my job. When she returned, I would have to show her the good time I had promised. This was supposed to be a celebration after all.

In preparation, I shot off the couch and skated to the kitchen, pouring us two more cups of the punch she had guzzled. She arrived by my side just after I finished, taking one of the drinks from my hand. "To you, Pinkie. And to my celebration today, of which we won't speak because that is part of my other life, not this one."

Something had changed since she had gone to the bathroom. When she'd walked away, her body was tense. Now, her eyes were bright. I wouldn't say she had relaxed, but the tension in her shoulders had traveled to the tips of her fingers and transformed to activity.

I would have to get her on skates some time.

No. I wouldn't. Stop it, Casey. This was it. Tonight. I couldn't be thinking about a future that would never happen. Next week I moved on to Alexandria and Baltimore after that. And then... who knew? I didn't have time or the energy to devote to a pretty, smart girl. Not long term.

Be here. Now. Today.

I lifted my cup. "To living life to the fullest."

"I'll drink to that." Our cups popped together. She kept her eyes on mine and I kept mine on hers as we drained the liquid courage.

I set my empty cup on the table. "So there *is* a party girl in there somewhere, huh?"

"Yep. I found her back near my college years. Wanna dance?"

"I would never tell a girl no to dancing."

I thought we would start dancing right there. The kitchen had mostly cleared out, and there was plenty of space. But Lips took my hand and pulled me into the living room where a tight knot of people jumped together singing along to a '90s grunge song. Before we even stopped, Lips let go of my hand. She closed her eyes and waved her arms in the air, becoming part of the music, her body an instrument the notes seemed to play.

On my skates, I needed lots of room to dance, and there was no room here. What could I do but watch her as her body slinked back and forth in her orange dress? She had shed her jacket, leaving her arms bare. She looked like she did yoga or lifted weights or something. She looked wonderful.

Now, I swayed with her, like an eel caught in quicksand, not exactly graceful, but what the fuck did I care? I closed my eyes and let the music take me like it was obviously taking my new friend. In the next moment, she wrapped her arms around my waist and dragged me forward until our bodies ground together.

Holy shit. If this was going to happen, and it felt like it was, I needed stability.

I pushed away, rolling backward. "Let me take off

my skates."

She opened her eyes, keeping them half-lidded, which only drove me crazier. "Does this mean it's a special occasion?"

"That's up to you, sweetheart," I said, bending over my wheels.

Never in the history of my skates had it taken so long to fucking unlace them. As I fumbled with them, Lips drew a finger over my spine. It sent a shiver straight down my backside and to my core. "If you want to keep your finger, you'll stop," I called, struggling out of my skates, feeling off balance.

She giggled. "Who needs fingers?"

"Everyone?" I said, successfully unlacing my other boot and ripping it off. There was something different about her. Something looser. The alcohol must be hitting her harder than me, or maybe she had had more to drink earlier than I'd thought. I shoved my skates between a pair of dancers and under a table.

Lips grabbed me by the hips and spun me around and now I was shorter than her by almost half a foot. I slid my arms around her neck and she slid her hands behind my back and she leaned her forehead on mine. The music danced in and around us. It changed to a more up-tempo number. Our movements quickened in pace, but we didn't break apart. If anything, we grew closer. Our hips locked in a rhythm both of us seemed already to know. My insides warmed, burned along with every point of my body touching hers. I wanted to be filled by her more than anything.

I broke first with a tiny tilt of my face up to hers.

She took my lips like they belonged to her. I wrapped my leg around her and she picked up my other one. With those strong yoga arms she carried me until we met with a wall. Then she pushed against me with all her strength. She was sweaty, or maybe I was sweaty. I didn't know.

She broke away. "Woohoo," she yelled, throwing her arms up in the air. My legs slid down and I jumped off her before something unfortunate like falling on my ass happened. She took one step around me and hopped up on the table, swinging her hips in a circle. Her fingers trailed along the hem of her dress.

Now people were starting to stare at her. Hell, I had stopped moving and started to stare. At first, in attracted wonder, with a lingering lust deep inside. Then, my attraction turned to horror as the dress wandered beyond her thighs to reveal a lacy set of cheeky underwear.

"Hey. Lips." Shit. Now I wished I knew her real name so it wouldn't sound ridiculous to yell in that moment. Had she taken something in the bathroom? No way she had gotten so drunk so fast. I reached for her hand, feeling soberer than I had all night. "Why don't you come down off the table?"

She whined and pulled her hand away. "Come on, don't be a buzz kill," she slurred.

I turned to face the gathering crowd. One of them had taken out her phone. Whoever the woman on the table was, she was the type of woman with a job. One that could be hurt if someone filmed her doing a little striptease on the coffee table.

Every part of me wanted to walk away. To leave

her here. When I'd invited her, I hadn't actually imagined I would be babysitting her, unless she was into that sort of thing. But I couldn't leave her here, either. Basic decency and all.

In my stockinged feet, I stepped up onto the coffee table and scooped her into my arms. She flailed, but I was strong enough to keep a hold on her and somehow managed to get us both down to the floor. She fought me all the way through the living room, through the gawking people. I let her down by the door because I couldn't hold her any longer.

"Stop it," I hissed. God, I should have known. Hadn't I learned my lesson that pretty girls were never worth the trouble? Pretty, wound up girls who couldn't have fun without getting smashed out of their minds were even more dangerous. This one had just killed every ounce of buzz in my body. She'd made me into her mother. The last thing I wanted to do was be anyone's mother.

She seemed to calm after my sharp words. She muttered things to herself. She probably couldn't get home on her own. Crap. *Why—why—did I invite her?* I opened the door and gently ushered her outside into the hallway so we could talk in peace.

"Did you drive?" I asked.

"Uber," she said. Little puffs of breath made her flyaways lift off her face. The fluorescent light of the hallway stripped away any illusion of sexiness—she was the color of grass in winter.

"I'll walk you outside to get a cab," I said, my hand on the small of her back.

"Don't." She pulled away, swerving to the edge of

the hall. "Don't touch me," she said more clearly. Her hair looked darker in this light, greasier with the sweat at her temples. We moved down the hall together. She worked hard at walking straight, but I remained vigilant. How did this get so bad so quickly? She'd only had one or two of those punch drinks, right? She must have had something else.

She used the wall as a support as she moved down the hall. She wasn't only drunk. This was different. Her hand, when I touched it, felt clammy. Her pulse fluttered in her wrist.

My own heart beat in my throat and my ears, spilling its worry into my head. What if she passed out or had a heart attack or something? I didn't even know her name.

"Is there anyone I can call for you? A sibling, maybe, a friend?"

A laugh burbled from her mouth. "God, no. No friends. No one can..." she trailed off.

I pressed the button for the elevator and waited with her, not pushing her to keep talking. She leaned heavily on my arm for support. At least she seemed calmer now, less combative.

The elevator dinged, and I stepped in with her. She held her stomach and turned a deeper shade of green. I said a silent prayer she would keep it together until we left the apartment building. She seemed to think the same, as when the elevator door opened, she broke into a run and disappeared out the front door.

When I followed her, I found her puking over a retaining wall into a bush.

Attractive.

Sighing, I walked over and picked up her clutch from the middle of the sidewalk and stuck it into the back of my shorts so no one wandering the streets could just pick it up. Then I gathered her hair at the nape of her sweaty neck and rubbed her back as she coughed up whatever she had in her stomach. Seriously? Seriously?

I'd spent far too much of my childhood taking care of stupid adults. I didn't want to spend my time doing that any longer. I was done. This was *my* trip. *My* time.

The woman finished and eased herself down to sit on the wall, hugging her arms under her legs. She sighed. "I'm so sorry," she said, her face pale, her eyes dull. "I always ruin everything."

I couldn't bring myself to sit down next to her, to tell her it was okay. That was a step too far, a step or seven beyond what I was willing to give. She was old enough to know her limits. My compassion only stretched to people who deserved it. "I'll hail you a cab."

"Wait," she said, drawing a shaking hand across the back of her forehead. "Could you… could you hold me for a minute? I'm so cold."

She must have left her jacket upstairs. I could see the goose flesh rising on her arms. In that moment, I felt myself grow hard.

"You'll be inside in just a minute," I said.

The night was lit by a bright moon and evenly spaced streetlights. The sidewalks were active with people streaming from bars. It had to be almost midnight, now. It didn't take long to find a cab, to open the door. Still in my socks, I walked over to her to help her to the car, guilt riding on my shoulder for my attitude, but she was already standing. So soon after puking in the bushes, she had managed to gather a bit of herself back. It almost looked like it had never happened. She pulled her shoulders back and offered me a smile that came nowhere near to touching her eyes.

She nodded once and slipped into the car. She made no move to kiss me, or hug me, or acknowledge any piece of intimacy we had shared inside. *Thank God.* She got in the car, I closed the door, and the car sped away.

There was nothing to mourn. There had been nothing between us except an electrifying spark. We obviously had nothing in common. She cared about her appearance, I didn't. She couldn't party without going overboard, I could. She was uptight, I fluttered in the wind. So why this twinge of sadness at the thought of never seeing her again?

I wandered back to the apartment building, slipping into my temporary home. Maybe I would leave D.C. sooner than I'd planned. It was full of people like that woman, complicated people, and I'd had enough of complicated people to last me a lifetime. I didn't need more.

I wandered through the lobby and to the elevator. After pressing the button, I shoved my hands into my back pocket.

No, no, no.

It was her wallet. I'd forgotten to give it back to her. How had I forgotten to do that? It was foolish, but I ran outside, like I was fucking Usain Bolt and could outrun the traffic. My skates often made me feel that way, but I was definitely skateless, and as I ran down the streets, I realized I could step on a pebble or a nail or a piece of glass and be out of commission for weeks, so I slowed.

In the light of the streetlights, bright as day, I unclasped the silver button of her simple black clutch and opened it. Through a plastic window, the woman stared back at me. The woman had a name. Savannah Burns.

It turned out I would have to see her one more time.

Chapter 5

SAVANNAH

The first three things I became aware of were the voices prattling in the hallway, my dry mouth, and my throbbing temples. The next was the kink in my neck, and the fact that my pillow had turned into a concrete slab overnight. Opening my eyes would only intensify the throbbing to bass drum levels, so I lifted and turned my head and rested it on the cool, hard surface instead.

Where am I?

I was lucid enough to realize I was sitting up now, which meant I wasn't at home. Our home was sparse and unless I had set up at the kitchen table for the night—no. There was no smell of food or coffee, just of… what? Carpet. Nothing?

My hands braced on the desk as I lifted my bowling ball of a head and squinted open my eyes.

Darn. I was at the office. How had I made it there?

I blinked. I remembered leaving the night before and heading into Shaw to meet that girl at the party. My vision was blurry, so I clawed around the top of my desk for my clutch. Where were my glasses? I was always losing my glasses. Lori had even bought me one of those necklace things to hang them on, but it made me look like a librarian so I'd never worn it. If only I had been able to get over my vanity, maybe I wouldn't be having this problem right now.

The throbbing in my head wasn't so bad as long as I kept my eyes mostly closed. It didn't even come close to comparing to the quicksand feeling of the air. I was swimming against the current, fighting for every movement. I needed something to pick me up real quick… to…

"You look like shit. Did you spend the night here?"

A blurred approximation of Lori folded her arms and leaned against the door frame. My mind went over what she had asked. I hadn't made it home last night… but how had I made it here? And where was my stuff? "Must have fallen asleep."

Lori stalked into the office, dropping her bag by her desk. Why was she always in my space everywhere I went? And where was my stuff? I opened the top drawer of my desk and rummaged around for a moment before pulling out a set of my old glasses and setting them on my nose. That was better. A little, at least. I could actually see now. Lori stood and flipped on the overhead light.

"Agh." I blocked my eyes. "Please, turn that off. You know I hate overheads."

"Are you ill?" Lori asked.

Through my arms, I watched as she moved closer.

"I'm fine." I stood. "I just need some coffee."

I must have stood too fast as the room swirled and tilted around me. I slowed so I wouldn't fall, but not enough to alert Lori to my extreme hangover. *Get it together, Sav.*

"Do you need help?"

"I'm not an old lady," I snapped, instantly feeling bad for my tone. I stopped at the door. "I'm sorry, Lori, just give me a minute to wake up, okay?"

"You better pull together before Tim comes in. He wants to meet with us at ten."

I nodded. She was right. Tim was our boss and he, though he didn't always show it, could always suss out when something was wrong. Using the wall, I made my way to the kitchenette, the long row of hallway overhead lights searing my brain. Whoever invented those things deserved a thorough torture session. They were horrible, horrible things. Ugly. Fake. They made everyone and everything look like death.

Pieces of the night before trickled back as I traversed the hall. I'd arrived at the party, and Pink intercepted me before I could leave. Then I started drinking that punch… it was all a blur after that. At the thought of Pink, something deep in my gut purred.

Had we…? Had we… Lord, I hoped not. That was the last thing I needed.

Thankfully, no one was in the kitchenette to talk to me, and I poured myself a cup of coffee. Its bitterness sharpened my focus and gave me back just a bit of myself. Unfortunately, that piece was not great. It could focus only on trying to fill in the night before, like my mind was a puzzle I had to put back together. Music. Pounding music. I'd danced with Pink.

That was bad enough. A better woman would have gone home to Lori, would have sat next to her in bed and watched her reality TV show with her. A better person wouldn't feel like her skin was melting off her at just the thought of that. It just seemed so mundane. But what was so bad about mundane? Lori was a wonderful woman. Pink had just been a fantasy. A fun… thing. My mind almost said fling, but I hoped to God it wasn't that.

Sex would be a betrayal. The worst kind of betrayal. Even with a couple of drinks in my system, I didn't think I would have done that.

I downed what remained of my coffee in one gulp and poured another. But there wasn't enough coffee in the world to pull me out of my funk today. I would just have to bootstrap the operation. To pretend. I wasn't bad at that. It was my specialty. I pretended all the way through college at Smith. All the way through law school. To pass the bar. That was all another Savannah. A better Savannah, though she wasn't real. Little Ms. Teen Louisiana Savannah. Today was no different. I just had to pretend.

For good measure, I downed another cup. It gave me enough strength to walk out into the hall with a smile and some of my trademark determination.

"Savannah, how are you this morning, my dear?" Tim's voice boomed like thunder in my ear.

It took all my strength not to flinch. "You're in a good mood today."

"It's a good day," Tim said. "It's the day we've been waiting for, and my sources tell me it's all going to go our way. I knew you could do it. I knew it."

I rarely met Tim's enthusiasm level, but today it was even worse. Today was the kind of day that would make me swear off alcohol for a while. I was getting too old for raging, and my body wasn't bouncing back like it did when I was twenty. I offered him a smile, though, because if I didn't give him just a little he would ratchet up his intensity level like it would somehow rub off on me.

"Thanks, Tim. My team deserves all the credit."

"I highly doubt that based on your performance last night. Lori told me all about it." Tim slapped me on the back.

I jumped and swallowed, my stomach rolling with the force of his hand. Holy balls of fire. How was I going to make it through this day? I stopped, holding my stomach.

Tim didn't seem to notice. "Meet me in the conference room as soon as you're ready."

I barely managed an "okay" before I ran to the bathroom and emptied my stomach of its contents. Hunched over the toilet, my throat burned raw with the bitterness of coffee, another image came to me. One of vomiting in a bush. A *bush*. I could only pray it wasn't on a busy street, and that I hadn't embarrassed myself too thoroughly.

As I washed my hands at the sink, I took a look at myself in the mirror. I looked ten years older than my age, I really did, and it wasn't just the horrid neon lights in the bathroom. And what did I have to show for it?

The door to the bathroom slammed open. "They're voting now. Come on, hurry," Lori said.

I pulled a paper towel from the hanger. "They're not due to vote until three."

"They moved it up."

"Why?"

"I don't know. I'm not a mind reader. Stop being so grumpy and come." Once Lori's words may have come in the form of a quip, but now they were sharp as a knife. She let the door swing shut just as I started moving toward it. I took another moment to make sure my stomach was done convulsing, then left.

First, I stopped in our office to look for my clutch again. It had everything. My phone, wallet, ID —everything—and I couldn't seem to find it this morning. It clearly wasn't on my desk, nor was it under the desk or in any of my drawers. My stomach dropped as I figured where it may be. At the party. I must have left it at the party.

Could I find that house again? I checked my arm. The address was too faded, impossible to read. Would my stuff still be there? My mind traced the route I'd taken to get to Shaw. It had taken, what? Thirty minutes, at least. Thirty back.

If the vote was happening and I was absent, I would never hear the end of it. It would have to wait. I changed into my spare dress and crept toward the conference room.

The room was plain, nothing special. Beige walls, a beige drop-tiled ceiling, stained brown in the corner. A white board covered with the yeas and nays, and Post-its clinging to every wall. About a dozen people filled the room—everyone from researchers, to the lobbyists on my professional level. Most of them were either on their phones or watching the vote with bated breath like it was the final inning of a one-run game of the World Series.

As I took my seat, I thought, it kind of was a

game, wasn't it? A high stakes game that could determine whether people got the care they needed or not, whether they were allowed in the country or not, the state of our environment. But it was still a game with rules.

I knew this. Mastering the game had allowed me to excel. Hopefully it had also caught Tim's eye. Hopefully it would get me the promotion I craved. I needed.

It was the next step.

No one engaged with me around the table as the votes came in. One after the other, representatives with whom I'd negotiated voted in a predictable fashion. If they hadn't, we wouldn't have been doing our jobs well. By the time the last vote was counted, we already knew we had won, but we all waited nonetheless. Silent.

As soon as the vote was announced the room erupted in cheers. Lori hugged Tim first, then made her way through the rest of the people to me. She hugged me and pulled away after a few seconds.

"Good job, Savannah." She patted me on the shoulder and turned.

We won. We'd finally passed environmental legislation that could change the world, I told myself. I should care about this. This was my baby, or it had been for the last few months. It could mean saving human kind. Intellectually, I knew this, but physically I didn't feel it. I felt nothing except a dull ache in the pit of my stomach. Nothing. Maybe this wasn't what I wanted after all. Maybe I had just been after the promotion. Could I be so shallow?

Absolutely. Did it matter?

The noise of the room was too much for my aching brain, so I slipped out without anyone noticing me. Or that's what I thought.

"Can I speak with you for a moment?" Tim asked, running to catch up with me. His workout routine must have been stellar. He was in marathon shape, maybe even Ironman shape. Just then, I noticed Lori on the other side of him.

"It's great, isn't it?" I said it because I knew I was supposed to think like that. It's not like I had always been like this—had I? When Pink had asked me what my favorite thing to do was I couldn't answer. *This* had been fun. Once. It was now, sometimes. Why not all the time any longer? Maybe I needed a new challenge.

"Yes, it's wonderful, and it's why…" he took my arm. "Come with me."

I followed him into a nearby room. Lori trailed behind. Tim slowed enough to close the door after us. This was it. He was going to tell me he was promoting me to partner, a position that would give me influence within the firm, not to mention the glory of being the youngest partner ever.

Tim leaned on his desk while Lori leaned on the back of the chair next to me. I stood straight, ready for what was to come. Readying myself to react properly.

A smile fluttered over Tim's lips and died. "I'll get right to it. You're a valuable part of this organization, Savannah, and you, too, Lori."

Lori? My mind traced the trajectory of this moment. Lori was *here*, which meant this wasn't about a promotion just for me. Maybe he was giving it to both of us? Like a team? Like I'd told her at the restaurant the night before?

"Did you know they're calling you The Closer, Savannah?" Tim asked.

"They? Who's they?" Heat met my cheeks, but I pushed it away. Couldn't let it get to my head.

"Other lobbyists. Legislators. You're an absolute shark, and I love it. That's why—"

"I accept."

Tim hesitated, the fingers of one hand tented on his desk as he leaned on it. For looks, more than function. "Oh, did you hear about our new client?"

"No, I just…" *Idiot. No. More. Alcohol.* "I'm willing to do whatever you need."

"Excellent. Well, I'm sure the Chalmont Foundation will be happy to hear that."

Chalmont Foundation. What did they have to do with my promotion? My brain was working so slowly it took me a few seconds to realize what he was talking about. The Chalmont Foundation—the foundation fighting against drug addiction. They had a bill coming out of committee.

My earlier words rose from my stomach, and I choked on them as they reached my throat. Why had I said I'd do *anything*?

"Are you all right, Savannah?"

"Yes." I pressed my fingers into my eyes. "I'm not feeling well today."

"Do you need to go home? Take the day?"

"No, no, I'm fine," I said, steadying myself on the edge of the desk. Partners didn't take sick days after partying. So, he wasn't giving me a promotion. He was giving me another case. "Brief me."

As Tim told me about the opioid epidemic and the importance of this legislation, I drifted away. Drifted to a place faraway from here, deeper south. A place with ghosts and dead people and tears and heartbreak and a whole lot of nothingness. Could I go back to that world?

"Savannah?" the deep voice was distant, like it was in a dream.

C'mon, Savannah. You've wanted this forever. I nodded, as if to myself and Tim. "Let's do this."

"Excellent. We'll have your annual review after you're finished with the case and see where things go from there." Tim clapped me on the shoulder, threatening the unsettled nature of my stomach, and left the room.

Lori stay behind, lingering like a shadow next to me. "What was going on with you there?"

"Nothing."

"Don't lie to me, Savannah. I know you better than that and I could see you struggling."

Leave it to Lori to notice this now, rather than the thousands of times I'd asked for her attention. I swallowed down a bunch of sour retorts about phones and television screens sucking her in.

"I better get back to work," I said, moving out of the room, hoping soon I would feel a little more like life rather than warmed over death.

Chapter 6

CASEY

Here were my options. Pretend I never found the wallet. Leave it with a local business. Send the wallet to the cops. Or bring it to Savannah at her work, or the place where her business card said she worked. So, really, I only had one option. Deliver the wallet— and Savannah's jacket which I had found trampled under a chair in the apartment—to her office. Personal delivery.

By the time I got my act together, it was mid-morning on Friday, which meant Savannah Burns would most likely not be at her home. She would be at the "Public Relations" firm Tim Wheeler and Associates in Capitol Hill. She was that type of girl. Woman. Whatever. A seven-to-nine type of woman. That explained a lot.

It took me a while to skate down to where she worked, mostly because of the slew of tourists clogging the sidewalks and pathways through the parks. Though wasn't exactly happy I had to deliver Savannah Burns's purse, once I broke free I couldn't help but smile. My skates made me feel like I was flying. I couldn't be unhappy on them.

After that, whenever I encountered a batch of tourists, I would sing out an "excuse me." Like the Red Sea, they would part the way and I would dance through.

Once, a little girl yelled "Mommy, look!" as I passed.

I turned around and blew her a kiss as I skated backward, swerving side to side in a dance. That right there was a major reason I did this. To show people—to show little girls, especially—you didn't need to take life so seriously. You could still have fun, even when you were a grown-up. It was a small thing, but a real thing, too. Happy people treated others with respect. Miserable people treated others like crap.

I was a firm believer the world would be a better place if people were just happy and secure. And I was doing my little part on my skates. Hopefully, the joy would spread from me to others.

As I approached the brick building of Savannah Burns's office, I steeled myself. Even thinking about entering the corporate world slickened my palms. Not to mention, what would I say to her? *Nice dancing last night. You're hot and I'm leaving. Here's your purse—don't worry, you didn't puke in it.*

Today was my first full day in D.C., and I had plans for pictures at the Lincoln Memorial and on the National Mall. All I had to do was get through this and I could move on.

I contemplated removing my skates, but since it would be such a short visit, I decided not to.

A young, college-age woman with a French-twist looked up from her desk, then gave me a skeptical look all the way up and down my body. "Can I help you?" she asked.

It didn't seem like she really meant it, but I forced myself not to care. I would never see this woman again. "I'm looking for Savannah Burns."

Her look grew even more skeptical. "I'm not certain Ms. Burns is available for a drop-in."

"Could you check? I have something to give her."

"Can I tell her who's asking?"

I sucked in a breath, but then remembered she didn't know my name. Giving the woman Pink sounded stupid, and I hated sounding stupid in front of people I didn't know. "Can you point me toward her office? I'll really just be a minute. I don't even need to see her."

"I'm afraid that's not possible." The woman stood. "I'll call and see if she's expecting someone."

"She's not," I said, but the woman had already picked up the phone and turned away from me.

This place, though open, was making me claustrophobic. It smelled of… nothing. That was the problem. It was nothing. It was so boring I wanted to gouge my eyes out just being in here for a few seconds. Don't get me wrong, it was perfectly respectable. Perhaps it would give other people confidence, just not me.

I was tired of waiting. I had places to be, so, quiet as I could, I skated down the hallway and took a sharp right. People looked up with lazy eyes that sharpened with surprise. I smiled and waved, glancing around for an office or some sign to tell me where to find Savannah. Finally, I decided to stop at the next desk. It was manned by a bearded dude. "Can you point me toward Savannah Burns?" I asked, my thumbs around the straps of my backpack.

"Uh…" He pointed straight over my shoulder.

Savannah Burns leaned on a desk with her arms

crossed. She wore a different dress, navy this time, and she didn't look as terrible as I expected, given the night she'd had. A woman stood next to her, closer than people stand most of the time. She was shorter, with a choppy chestnut bob. I found myself eying her before I reminded myself I was here for one reason only. To return the clutch.

Sliding the backpack from my shoulders, I skated toward the doorway.

"Savannah?" I said, my mouth growing dry with her name.

She remained in the same position but twisted her head toward me. Her eyes registered nothing as she blinked once, then again. The Queen of Nothingness. The Queen of Emptiness. I would have to work on her new nickname over the course of the day.

"Yes?" she asked, breaking me from my trance.

"I have your purse. Here." I dug in my bag. "Somewhere, here…" I hadn't felt so embarrassed since I'd lost my registration for college classes almost five years ago. In fact, it had been a similar situation then, two beautiful women staring at me while I fumbled in my bag. That time, a hole had been the culprit. I'd lost half my stuff that day. This time, it was those dead slate eyes.

Miserable. She was one of those miserable people. She hadn't seemed like it when we'd met, but she did now given what I knew.

"Do you know her?" I heard the shorter woman whisper.

"No," Savannah said.

The word pierced my heart, though it shouldn't

have. She was right. She didn't know me. I didn't know her. We had shared mere moments together, and that was it. I finally located her damn clutch and jacket and walked over to her on my toes. The closer I got, the more my eyes went to those moles on her face, to her lips. The more my insides heated. No way. I wasn't doing this. Not now. Or ever.

"Thank you," Savannah said.

"Where did you find it?" the other woman asked. Her acorn-brown eyebrow quirked. She flicked a glance to Savannah and then back at me and that's when I knew… this woman was more than just a colleague. She might not even be a colleague. Maybe she was Savannah's partner. Of course. She had someone, and I had kissed her. It wasn't my fault. If anyone was cheating, it was Savannah, not me.

But I also wasn't going to ruin her life. That's not the kind of person I was. "I found it on the street outside. Must have dropped it."

I closed the distance to Savannah and gave her the clutch. The sooner I got out of there, the better. My skates were useless on the carpet and I didn't have any air. How did anyone breathe in the stale office air? I handed her the clutch, and our fingers accidentally brushed. In that moment, Savannah's hard silver eyes melted to something liquid and cool and… vulnerable. Was she scared?

If I didn't want to blow our cover, I couldn't hold the gaze a second longer or we would be found out, so I turned away from her and put physical distance between us. As I turned into the hallway, I realized I hadn't even said goodbye, which would probably be even more suspect. But what did I care? I was done.

Done.

"She was odd," I heard the other woman say as I skated away.

"Yeah," Savannah said, like we had shared nothing.

Done.

...

SAVANNAH

"Do you think she stole anything?" Lori asked. "Why don't you check?"

I could still hear the rolling of Pink's skates down the hallway. What had I done? I could have chosen a million ways to react. Even if she had been a stranger, others would have shaken her hand, thanked her profusely, but I'd acted like she'd given me a penny off the street, rather than my whole life back.

"It's all here," I said.

Of course it was. Even without looking, I knew she wouldn't steal anything. If she'd wanted to do that, she didn't have to show up here. She'd come because she wanted to see me. I could remember enough of last night's performance to wonder why. Unless I had slept with her.

Sex made you do some crazy things.

That, plus the way I had just treated her like dirt when all she'd done was be kind to me, drove me to take my next step forward. "Be right back," I said to Lori. "I'm going to freshen up."

As soon as I cleared the corner, I broke out in a run. Pink wasn't there, nor was she in the lobby. I slipped off my heels and burst outside only to catch her rummaging in her bag right next to the door.

"Hey," I said, surprised to see her so close.

She twisted her neck to face me. "So you're talking to me now?"

"I wanted to tell you I'm sorry. And thank you."

She straightened, cracking her back. "You already said that inside."

"No, I mean, thank you for taking care of me last night. I can't remember much of it, but from what I do remember, you were very sweet."

"It's nothing." Pink slung her backpack over her shoulder and started skating away in the other direction. Could I let her go? Just like that?

"Wait." I ran after her, instantly out of breath after my hard night. By the time I got to her, I had to brace my hands on my knees to catch my breath. But before she left, I had to know. I had to know whether I had crossed the line. "Wait, please."

She swung around, her face placid, unreadable as a mask.

I struggled for air, but I caught it soon enough. "Did we sleep together?" I asked bluntly, not one to tiptoe around the subject.

Pink rolled her eyes, a hard, empty laugh coming out of her mouth. "So that's why you left your pretty assistant and your sacred office and chased me down? Not to thank me."

"No, that's not it." None of this was coming out right. "I just need to know."

"Why? Is it so horrible to imagine?"

"No," I said, surprised by her sudden turn in temperament. "Not at all. I just. The woman back there—"

"Are you married?"

"Me?"

"Do you see me talking to anyone else?"

What was wrong with her? Had I done something to hurt her? "God, no. Not married. Just… just… living together."

Pink scoffed and turned, skating away.

This non-answer pissed me off more than anything. "How dare you judge me? You don't know my situation at all."

She waved a hand. "I know a coward when I see one."

I was so angry I could spit, and I practically did. "A coward? You know nothing about me."

"Whatever."

"Stop."

She let her skates roll to a slow stop. People streamed around her as if they were a current splitting around a stump in a flood. I caught up with her. "What do you mean a coward?"

She stared ahead.

"Look at me."

She met my gaze with her dark blue storm cloud eyes. Had they always been that blue or did they change when she was angry? All I knew was I had to see her when she told me whatever came next. "What makes you think I'm a coward?"

"I really should go," she said. "I've got a lot to do today."

I caught her hand before she could finish turning away. "Please. I want to know."

"Do you?"

"I'm asking."

The pull on my grip relaxed as Pink rolled closer to me. "I know people like you. Ambitious people. People who refuse to live *their* lives."

She was speaking words, but it sounded like another language altogether. They didn't make sense. "How can I do anything but live my life? Isn't that what we all do?"

"Sure. But there's tolerating life and then there's living and respecting it."

How much time had passed since I'd left the office? When would Tim be giving me the details of my new job? Soon, I would think. Lori would grow suspicious of my absence as well and that was the last thing I needed. "Can you stop with the malarkey, please, and tell me what you mean?"

"I'm not—" Pink sighed and turned away. "Why do I even bother?"

She infuriated me, irritated me, but she had also made me feel more alive than I'd felt in a long time, a little like young Savannah. She—this stranger—was my lifeline back.

"How would you like to quadruple your contributions to your charity project this weekend?" I called.

Pink jumped backward and skidded to a stop in less than a foot. The people around her sneaked glances at her skates, her outfit, her hair. She was so *her*. She tilted her head, regarding me for a moment. Unfortunately, I couldn't make myself look any less wretched in my day-old makeup and unwashed hair, but I did try to show her I was serious.

She skated toward me and I scrambled for something else to say to keep her there.

"As a thank you. For last night."

She stopped a few feet away from me. There might as well have been a chasm between us, though, for all her stiff body language. "You can quadruple my donations?"

"Maybe more. I promise I'll leave behind all the drama. No more alcohol for me for a while."

Pink looked away.

"If you need proof—"

"I believe you can, I'm just trying to figure out whether it's a good idea or not."

"Honestly? I would be thinking the same thing if I were you. Last night probably made me look like a hot mess, but I promise that wasn't the real me. I'm not usually like that."

Her gaze darted back to me. I was still groggy and wired at the same time, and I didn't try to hide any of it from her. I just let her see it. The lid over my left eye twitched.

She nodded. "Okay. Tomorrow. Meet me at the Butternut Café at eleven AM."

"It'll be my treat. It's a date," I said.

I couldn't be sure, but I thought I heard her say, "Yeah, maybe not so much," as she skated away.

Chapter 7

CASEY

If I'd learned one thing in my life of being bounced around from home to home, it's that life is better when you walk into situations expecting nothing. Then you couldn't be disappointed. Of course, sometimes, the situation was so bad you couldn't possibly lower your expectations more. I'd been in those circumstances, too, but not since I set out on my own.

As I approached the café where I was supposed to meet Savannah Burns, I considered if this was one of those situations. Again. I had been considering all night. Telling myself I would say no and skate away. That Savannah was trouble. Crack. Then berating myself for being selfish. Quadruple the money for the kids? And I was just going to run from that?

Certainly, no lasting harm would come to me from a meeting. In fact, it was possible only good could come from it.

This was for the kids. The kids.

My resolve weakened as I approached and caught sight of the woman in the picture window. She looked refreshed, relaxed, with her blonde hair straight and over her shoulders, her hands wrapped around a mug. She wore a three-quarter sleeve sweater the color of the Caribbean Ocean. I was about to skate right on by when she met my eyes and a smile caved in her cheeks.

Dimples. She had to have dimples. They were the worst. But if I wanted to remain unscathed in this, I had to remember to keep my head and my pants on straight.

For the kids.

With a breath, I opened the door and skated inside. The café was crowded with the morning brunch crowd. Hipsters, men in suits even on a Saturday. As usual, people stared, but I'd come to expect that nowadays and acted like I didn't care. I swerved over to Savannah in a wide arc, one foot in front of the other, and stopped short at the table.

"Good morning," she said, not blinking an eye, her dimples deepening. She wore no makeup except mascara on her dark lashes. Her eyes were a color I'd never seen in eyes before. Asphalt. The sea in winter. Yes. The oceans of the Pacific Northwest in winter. On a rainy day.

Ignoring the pull of my body, I took the seat across from her and picked up a menu so I wouldn't have to look at her. It was better that way. "What's cookin'?"

"I hope you don't mind," Savannah said. "I thought you might be hungry, so I ordered a little of everything for breakfast. Pancakes, eggs, French toast, the works."

Food. My mouth filled with water, betraying me just like the rest of my body. If Savannah Burns was trying to seduce me, doing so through my mouth wasn't a bad start. But why would she want to seduce me? She had a partner. I had to get my mind out of that gutter.

I thought about turning the food away, to set a firm boundary, but what was the point of wasting all that food? I put down the menu, sliding it to the edge of the table. "That sounds amazing."

Savannah bent her head, taking in a long sniff of her coffee. "Can I ask you a question?"

"Sure," I said, squaring my shoulders.

"What's your real name?"

I'd known hers long enough for it to burn its way into my mind. Get it? Burns? Oh God, I was making jokes to myself. I must be in real trouble. What was wrong with giving her my real name?

"Casey Day."

"It's very nice to meet you, Casey Day. I'm Savannah Burns." She held out a hand. I took it because what else was there to do? Her fingers brushed the sensitive spot on my wrist at the base of my palm and I dropped hers like a hot skillet.

Triple shit sandwich. Why had I done that?

The waitress appeared a moment later and poured some coffee into my mug. "Is there anything else I can get you?"

I needed something to relax me because whatever Savannah Burns was putting out had me on edge. All she'd done was ask my name, which made me think maybe I was doing this to myself. "A mimosa?"

The waitress winked. "You got it."

She turned to Savannah, who lifted her hand and shook her head. I remembered then what she'd said about swearing off alcohol and felt terrible for ordering, but by the time I realized, the waitress was already gone. "Sorry. I forgot."

"Pssh." Savannah waved and shook her head. "I wouldn't limit your fun. It's not like I'm an alcoholic, anyway. I just went overboard the other night."

"Are you… were you okay?"

"Yeah. It was just stupid. I was overwhelmed by the party and…" she waved her hand in front of her face. "It just got away from me."

It reminded me of the moment after she'd lost her drinks in the bushes, of when she had curled up and said she ruined everything. It was an extremely *human* moment. I'd been so busy judging her for getting out of control like that, for being uptight, for ignoring me, I'd forgotten. Of course she was human. "I hear you. That can happen when you're having fun, or when you're really not."

Savannah laughed and it sounded like a song. How was it possible everything she did was so perfect? Everything except party, I reminded myself. Right. The image of her puking in a bush brought me back to the current moment. Business. In. Out. Gone. "So, you think I can quadruple my donations? How?"

She shrugged, her slender shoulder popping out of her boat neck sweater. "You just need to tell a story."

I didn't actually believe she could do this. I'd been working my ass off for over seven months and was just inching along. "Aren't I already? I've been documenting my skate across the country."

"Yes." Savannah's face lit up. "And that's really cool, but that's only one piece of the story, the part people can easily see. There's got to be more, a reason you're doing this. Some personal reason.

People are always curious about motivations. What made you decide on foster kids as your focus?"

"I was one," I said simply. As I did, warmth crept up my neck like I'd been injected with it, and I was happy for the layer of makeup that would at least make the blush seem less extreme on my pale skin.

"That's great."

"Excuse me?"

"I mean, that's great for your cause. You have personal experience with this. You know what these kids are going through. That means you can empathize with them. Now all you have to do is to tell your story, to make people feel what you felt as a kid."

With skates on, it was hard to bounce my knees. The heavy trucks kept me glued to the floor. Instead, I rolled them forward until they hit the legs of the table in the middle, and back until they hit the bottom of the bench on which I sat. Forward—click —back—click. Fidgeting. That had always been a problem for me in school. There was no one to yell at me for it now, except myself. I stilled my movements. "I don't think people want to hear about that."

"Of course they do." Savannah reached out and took my hand. Mine rested like a wet fish under her strong grip. In an instant, questions flashed through my mind. What should I do? Flip it upward to hold her hand? Keep it here dead on the table? Tense it so it didn't seem so limp and sweaty? Pull it away? Gosh, when had been the last time I felt so uncertain? Flirting with a stranger was easy, but the moment the whiff of some stronger partnership formed, my nerves clamped down like a claw on my stomach.

Savannah kept speaking. "You are the American Dream."

I stared at our hands. A single syllable laugh fell from my mouth and died on the table. "Not exactly. I don't have any money."

Savannah squeezed. "It's not always about the money. It's about freedom."

My life as the American Dream? I would give anything for a *normal* life without this *dreamy* part of it if I could. But how would someone like Savannah understand that? She probably didn't know a thing about the foster care system. Why should she? If you could avoid it, you should, at all costs. It was too gritty. No one really wanted to know. "I appreciate what you're trying to do, but I really don't think it's going to work."

Savannah pulled her hand away and folded her arms under her breasts, accentuating them. "Tell me about it. What draws you to these kids? You don't have to tell your whole story, just make it a little personal. Weave in what you want."

Thankfully the food arrived before I had the chance to answer. Savannah had ordered so much for me we had to Tetris it all around the narrow booth table to make it fit.

I dug right in, starting with the scrambled eggs, which I ate in about a minute. I moved on to my favorite next. The slabs of Texas style French toast were smothered in strawberries and syrup and absolutely delicious. Only after a couple bites of those, when I was forced to pause so I wouldn't choke, did I look up and notice a pathetic plate of egg whites in front of Savannah. She was beaming at me. The bite in my mouth seemed too large, so I set down my fork and chewed until I could swallow. "Do you want some?" I asked, though I really didn't want to offer.

"No, I'm enjoying the show. You look like you love it too much to share."

I hesitated, then rolled my eyes in pleasure, leaning back on the seat, the sweet and tart taste of strawberries lingering on my tongue. "I do, especially because I don't know when I'll taste food like this again."

"We'll have to be sure to order some cinnamon buns to go, then. This café is famous for them."

I groaned, my mouth and stomach totally shipping me and Savannah—the traitors. "How do you know how much I love cinnamon buns?"

"Based on the way you're attacking those pieces of French toast? Just an educated guess." Savannah winked.

I cut a daintier piece and set it on my tongue, reminding myself to slow down. If I wasn't careful, the food would lull me into a sense of calm, and who knew what I would agree to then. *Marriage? Sure. I'd already sold her my soul. Why not?* Made perfect sense on a French toast high.

Savannah cut a tiny piece of her egg white as well and chewed it, though she obviously got no pleasure from it. I pushed my plate of French toast toward her. "You've got to try some of this. It's the best I've ever tasted. It's stuffed with cream cheese, too."

"Don't tempt me."

"Why not?"

"A bite of that will instantly add ten pounds to my hips."

"You could use it."

She turned away, biting down on her lips. That's all I needed. I sliced a generous portion of the French toast and speared it with my fork. "One bite isn't going to make you fat."

"You can say that because you're—"

I stuffed the bite in her open mouth.

Her lips closed around the fork and my breath caught in my throat as I watched her close her eyes and moan.

"Oh, Lord in heaven and the devil in hell," she said, her eyelids fluttering.

I barked a laugh. "Was that a southern accent?"

Savannah's shoulders came up to her ears as she covered her mouth and laughed and chewed. "I'm from Louisiana."

I closed my eyes and leaned my head back, images of my journey so far floating through my head. "Louisiana, huh? I can picture it now. A sprawling plantation house with a wrap-around porch and a willow tree with Spanish moss out in front. It must have been peaceful."

"Something like that."

Savannah's voice had a hard edge to it that made me open my eyes. "Did I say something wrong?"

"No—let me see your Instagram account again," she said, her palm up in an offering.

She was all business again. None of the pleasure I'd witnessed a few moments before remained, and I wasn't going to argue. That's what I had wanted, right? Not a social brunch where we intertwined arms and drank champagne and gossiped.

I fished my phone from my bag, opened the app, and set the phone in her palm. The dirty rainbow case clashed against her clean hands, but she didn't seem to mind. She scrolled through, nodding. I picked at my food, though it no longer looked as appetizing. What had happened in that moment to turn her from a smiling dimpled goddess back to the hard businesswoman? It was something about her home. Something I'd said.

She handed the phone back. "There are two things I would recommend. You do a lot of cool skating tricks, which would get the attention of skaters, but how many skaters do you know actually have money?"

I swallowed the bite in my mouth and set my hands in my lap, feeling a little like I was in school. I was never a good student—could never sit still. I'd been in so many schools, I'd never really had many friends either. "I don't know. Some. Maybe?"

"Probably not many. It's a small audience, anyway. So, you have to shift your target audience. You don't need people with a lot of money, just a lot of people with a little money willing to give to a good cause. You know what I like to do? I like to try my pitches out on my friends before I throw them to the world. If they work on the people you love, then you know you've found something that will at least touch someone. Here, watch."

Before I could protest, she dialed a number on her phone and set it between us. As the phone rang, she met my eye. "I'm calling my friend Alice. She's the sweetest of all my college friends and if she—"

"Savvy Sav, I'm so happy you called," a woman answered. She appeared on the screen, wearing a large bow headband, like a redheaded Alice in Wonderland. "How are you?"

"I'm great, sweetie." Sav leaned over so the woman on the other end could see her. "How are you?"

"Wonderful. Donald's here. Want to say hi?"

"Sure." Sav—I liked that nickname for her, it was easier—leaned away from the screen and whispered to me. "It's her pug. Rule one of getting something from someone—acknowledge their babies and dogs, even if you hate babies and dogs which would make you—"

A wrinkly pug face filled the screen. Sav tilted the phone toward her. "Oh, look at that adorable face. He is too much, Alice. Ugh. I can't wait to come to visit—"

"When?" The pug's face disappeared, replaced by the woman's face again. She wore about as much makeup as I did, which was saying something.

"Hopefully soon. I just completed a project, but Tim dropped another one in my lap. Maybe we can do another Club soon? With all the girls on video chat?"

"I'd love that."

"Me too."

My throat closed. I'd only witnessed a minute of conversation between these two, but I could tell they had a tight bond. I didn't have that with anyone, not that I wanted it. In my experience, relationships this close tended to blow up. They took work, and I wasn't good at that type of work. At least I knew it, right? I settled back in the bench, reaching for my glass of water to quench my suddenly dry throat.

"Hey," Sav said after a pause. "I'm actually calling for a friend. She's sitting right here, and she has something to ask you."

Sav shoved the phone in my face. Panic seized me. I could do a backflip off a ramp and not be scared. I could rappel into canyons. I could jump from planes. But this? This put me straight into cold-sweat territory. I rubbed my hands on my jean shorts to dry them and glanced up at Savannah, uncertain.

She rolled her hand.

"Hi," I said, my throat dry as the Sahara.

"Hi, I'm Alice."

I opened my mouth and closed it. Opened it again and scratched out my name. "I'm Casey."

"It's nice to meet you, Casey."

Yes, it was all nice and fine, but my heart was beating and my palms were sweating and a boa constrictor was starting to tighten around my lungs. Sav leaned over and touched my elbow again, her warmth adding to my full-on panic. "Try what I suggested. She won't say no."

"What can I do for you?" Alice asked.

Blank. My mind went blank. Blackness edged on my vision, blotting out half of Savannah's face. Why was she putting me in this position? I didn't have to be here. I didn't have to do this.

I slid out of the bench.

"What are you doing?" Savannah called.

"Aren't you going to pay?" the waitress asked as I skated by.

"I'll be right back, promise," I heard Savannah

say.

She followed me out the door and onto the street. I started skating, but we were in a busy section of town, and I had to keep my speed down on the sidewalk. *Damn it*, why had I agreed to meet her here? This may be the only case where meeting on a deserted park bench would have been smart on my part.

Savannah caught my elbow and drew me up short. "What are you doing?"

I ripped my elbow away from her grasp. "Don't ever put me in a position like that again."

"I was just trying to help."

"It's not helpful to force me to beg on the phone. It's condescending. It's—it's..." In an uncharacteristically clumsy moment, my skate flew out from under me. I spun in an effort to keep my balance but still fell backward. Savannah caught me under my arms. My heart thudded in my chest, probably from almost falling, but it didn't help that this beautiful girl had a grasp on me. Damn all the beautiful girls. Damn her.

"I'm sorry. I shouldn't have done that," Savannah said, whispering in my ear from behind me. "I just thought you could use a little practice asking for money. That's what you're doing here, right?"

"I was doing fine on my own."

"But you could do better."

My eyes flooded with tears. What the hell was happening to me? I never cried, not since I was little. Crying didn't help anyone. I blinked them back. "I'm sorry. I've gotta go."

Savannah released me as I stood on my own.

"I'm really sorry if I did something to hurt you. Please take care of yourself out there."

As I skated away, her words echoed in my mind. Not just their content, but their softness. She meant it. Savannah Burns wasn't just a southern belle with a cut-throat attitude and a party problem. She had a soft side. She had dimples. She was human. And she had cared. About me.

It was good thing I was leaving and not a moment too soon.

Chapter 8

SAVANNAH

How was I supposed to know a simple phone call would be too much?

I watched Pink as long as I could, her pigtails sticking up into the air like a grown-up Pebbles. She was so unlike any woman I'd ever met. Both childish and grown-up. Sexy, yet fragile. She kept surprising the ordinariness out of me, and as I watched her skate away, I imagined for a second what my life would be like if I forgot about this work stuff and went with her.

I imagined us holding hands and skating on an empty tree-lined road. I imagined Pink wrapping her arm around my back and me swinging around and kissing her as we rolled, me backward, her forward.

Ha. Was I dreaming or what? The last time I skated had been at Ashley Borrough's eighth birthday party, and it was indoors, and I'd spent more time clinging to the wall along the edge of the rink than rolling free. That had been before everything collapsed with my family. Before my parents became ghosts, and I was the only one left alive. The fact that Pink—Casey—actually made me even imagine myself doing that was compelling in itself.

She disappeared into the crowd, but that, for

some reason, only fed my longing. I gave myself a minute—one minute only—to dream about a life with her. How joyful it could be. Could feel. Unfettered by jobs or deadlines or walls. Off the game board entirely, traveling around the country, seeing all the places I'd always wanted to see.

But that was only a dream. I had important things to do here. A calling. A life.

I ambled back into the café and settled our bill. Then I called Alice back and apologized for what happened, telling her I would explain when I had the chance.

I couldn't bring myself to return home quite yet, so I went to work and started to dig into the materials on opioid abuse. I looked at it objectively, studying the statistics for each state, figuring out which legislators would be best to target, the science behind addiction and abuse. It helped to pretend I was that other Savannah for this. It helped to focus on the numbers as numbers and not think of them as people.

Though eventually, I would have to look at the people. Stories of real life suffering would be the only thing to make the American public *care*. Numbers weren't good enough. I had to bring out the stories. But not today.

The shadows lengthened over my desk until I could no longer see anything beyond my laptop without turning on my lamp. I stretched, my mind wandering. What kind of laws were there to protect foster care kids? I did some research. The anecdotal and social science evidence was pretty dire there, too. Some organizations estimated only half graduated high school, and three percent graduated college. There were reports of terrible situations, but even well-meaning foster parents often didn't have the resources to provide for their kids. Plus, once they hit eighteen, they were on their own.

What had Casey been through? What had happened to her that forced her into the system in the first place?

Maybe, after the opioid bill, I could look into foster care. They were related, after all. If I got this promotion, I could certainly suggest it. Work from *within* the system rather than without. That was the way to make a difference.

Speaking of operating from within, if today had taught me anything, it was that I had some work to do on my relationship with Lori. If I was having these feelings for someone else, these daydreams, wasn't it a sign we weren't doing well? As if I needed another sign.

Instead of staying the extra three hours I might have on another Saturday night, I packed up and set off for home. Home was a small apartment I shared in a narrow periwinkle row house with Lori in the Navy Yard neighborhood of D.C. When I walked in, downstairs was silent. I set my bag in the hall and pulled my hair out from its messy bun. Then I walked up the stairs to our bedroom and leaned on the door frame.

Lori reclined on our rumpled, unmade bed. She didn't look up at my approach. Maybe she hadn't heard me.

"Hey, Lor. How was your day?"

"Ummm…" her eyes flicked to me, a questioning

arch developing in her brow, before her gaze returned to her computer screen. "Fine."

My stomach clenched and my fists clenched and everything clenched as I prepared for a snappy reply, but I was trying to be better. Right? Make the system better. Make *me* better. Better meant patience. "Do you want to have dinner out tonight?"

"I'd rather not change out of my yoga pants right now."

Or do anything else, apparently. Knowing Lori, she'd slept in what she was wearing. She probably hadn't showered that day. How could she go so long doing absolutely nothing? "Maybe I'll make some spaghetti and meatballs? Your favorite?"

Lori's eyes, just her eyes, tracked mine. The reddish glow of her screen lit her face as if it wanted to pull her in. "Thanks, but I already ate a ton today and I'm feeling super bloated. I don't think I'll have dinner tonight."

Son of a… this woman wasn't making things easy. I tried to remember back to the old days, what we used to be like. How had we first connected? It was at work. We'd been flirting for quite some time and had a secretive tryst in the copy room and then… what? We'd ended up here? Living together? For more than a year? What did we have in common? I liked to be active, she liked to stay on the couch. I liked social things, she didn't.

It was the sex. That's what it was. When we'd had it, it had been mostly good, but we hadn't had it in months.

I fingered the bottom of my sweater and pulled it over my head. Then I strode over to her and crawled onto our king-sized bed, a bed I hadn't touched in quite some time. I placed my palm on the laptop cover and closed it.

"What are you doing?" Lori put her hands on my chest and pushed me away as I kissed her on the lips and dragged her laptop out from underneath me.

"I'm kissing my incredible girlfriend," I said, testing the words on my lips. They seemed true enough. Arguably, she was incredible at certain things.

She squirmed under me. "Come on. I haven't even brushed my teeth yet," she said, pulling her face away.

"I don't care," I said, cupping her face in my hands. "I don't care if you haven't showered in days, if you haven't brushed your teeth or your hair or shaved your legs. I just—I want you."

A deep hunger was taking hold of my insides, a need. Like a baby bird it demanded food, squawking and doing my head in. She fought me, and not in a sexy way. I kept trying to kiss her, my chest pecked raw by the baby birds, my breath shortening. She slid out from under me and crouched on the end of the bed, her forest green eyes daggers of hate.

Hate.

"Come on, Lori. Please." I detested the begging in my voice. Since when did I have to beg for sex?

"No."

"Seriously?" I reached out, but she backed away like I was coming at her with a knife rather than with my love.

"What's wrong with you?" I snapped.

"I don't want to have sex. Is that a crime?" Her

wide eyes were even bigger than usual. Her hair lank.

"Of course not," I bit out. "But it's been months, Lori."

"No… that's not possible."

"When was the last time? Tell me exactly."

Lori stared at our sunshine walls, too bright for the moment, and didn't seem to notice them as her eyes moved from side to side. She may have had a brain for numbers, but not for people. Not for relationships. Not for significant events in temporal time. That's why I handled the interactions with the people and she developed the strategy based on the numbers. "I can't remember," she said.

I could, but it wasn't because it was memorable. In fact, it was the opposite. A quickie where both of us had been elsewhere. I only remembered because I remembered stuff like that. "Almost a year ago."

I let that settle in, but Lori shook her head. Then she shrugged. "I don't feel like it right now."

"Then when?"

"I don't know."

"Can we set a date?"

Lori blinked, frowning. "Don't you think it should be spontaneous? Isn't that more romantic?"

"Anything would be more romantic than this. We barely see each other. Come on. I'll make you dinner. You can take a shower or a bath, or whatever you need to get in the mood. Maybe I'll bust out the toys…"

Lori gazed at her computer with more longing than she had displayed for me in a long time. I suppressed the urge to pick the darn thing up and throw it across the room, smashing it against the wall. She wasn't even pretending any longer. I leaned over and pulled the overnight bag from under the bed. "I can't be here."

"Where are you going?" Lori asked, finally scrambling off the bed. "Are you seriously leaving because I won't have sex with you? Don't you think that's a little shallow?"

Lori followed me throughout the apartment as I gathered some things, peppering me with these questions.

"I just need some space," I said.

"You have space. You're barely ever home. You leave me here all day, all weekend, and every night, and come home and just expect me to perform? Demand sex? I mean, you didn't even give me any warning."

"I expect you to love me," I said, whirling around, my trench coat over one arm and my bag over the other. "I expect you to pay attention to me sometimes when I'm here. For a few minutes, even."

"That's not fair."

I shrugged. "Maybe it's not, but it's common decency, isn't it? I'm trying here. And what could possibly be more important than us?"

Lori didn't seem to have an answer to this. That was it. I had to leave before I did something I would regret. I turned for the door.

"Where are you going?"

"I don't know. Away."

"Will you call me when you get there?"

"I'll text you when I'm safe." I opened the door and closed it behind me. It wasn't the sex. It had never been about the sex. It was about the fundamental foundation of the relationship. Lori was a stranger, even more strange than the real stranger currently in my life. Casey. And, without even challenging it directly, Casey had made me see what I'd been ignoring for far too long. She reminded me what it was like to feel.

Operating within the system, in the realm of my relationship, had just become impossible.

Chapter 9

CASEY

You know what was wrong with Savannah Burns?

She was pushy. Pushy and irritating and self-righteous and wound up and knotted so tight she was going to have to find an awful big pair of scissors to set herself free.

The night after my disastrous meeting with Savannah, I sat in Denise's empty apartment on the very couch where Savannah and I had kissed for the second time and stared at my computer screen. She had been wrong about how I should approach this. I could never sit and make phone calls to people, even people I knew. That just wasn't me.

But looking at my social media accounts with fresh eyes, I realized, begrudgingly, she was right about something.

I'd spent the night studying accounts of successful female entrepreneurs and fundraisers and tried to figure out which of their causes I was most inclined to give to. I took notes on tactics they used. Begging. Contests. Stories. Creating a tribe.

And the stubborn, pushy woman was right.

The best ones told stories.

There was a lot about skating on my accounts, but not a whole lot about the kids in the system. I wasn't telling a story. Had I done this selfishly? No, I didn't think so. I *was* donating all the money, after all.

But whose story would I tell? The kids who most needed our attention were often exploited and used. I didn't want to do use them for that, too. Even if it was for their own good.

Which meant I had to tell *my* story.

Doodling on a scrap piece of paper, I tried to figure out what I would tell them. *I do this because I was a foster kid*, was too bland, not personal enough. Even I could see that.

I settled into the couch and closed my eyes. What did it feel like to be homeless, parentless? To have nothing in the world to call my own, not even a tooth brush or a blanket? Chills ran down my arms, though it was plenty warm in the apartment. A salty bile clogged the back of my throat.

God, even asking sent me into a cold sweat.

Before I thought myself into a fit, I turned on the recorder on my phone and set it at eye level. I swallowed down the fear rising up and reminded myself this was for the kids. I could do this for them. I could do anything for them.

"When I was seven," I said, my palms oozing sweat. "I was put into the foster care system. They only let me bring my bear with me. I had to leave everything else behind. The first house I was in—" I swallowed, but no matter how much I swallowed, I could no longer speak past the lump.

I turned off my recorder. It was too much. I couldn't talk about my story, it just… I wasn't ready yet. What would people say? Some people knew about my past, but I never used it as an excuse for my life.

Maybe a picture would do better.

I took a selfie and added a pink and blue filter to it.

Underneath I wrote.

When I was young, my seventh-grade teacher took an interest in me when I needed it most. I'd graffitied her desk. She gave me detention, but instead of making me clean the marker off her desk, she wrote an address on a piece of paper. It was her home address. She told me I could write whenever I wanted, and she became my one constant for the next years as I moved from foster home to foster home. She made me feel loved, anchored. Unfortunately, the world lost her too young, but I hope to carry on her legacy. That's why I'm skating the country as a challenge for an organization called Voices for Love. They give a bag of things to kids when they enter the system, and assign them a pen pal. You all should join.

Be there for a kid. If you can't give your time, give your money. You never know what will touch someone's heart. Xo. Casey. #tellyourstory #mywordsmatter

Before I could doubt it, before I could edit out the heart, I posted it to Instagram and Facebook. Then I shut off my computer and phone. My hands trembled, my breath caught, but it wasn't like earlier. It wasn't fear. It was excitement. I'd put myself out there and it was terrifying and exhilarating as anything I'd ever done.

Whatever happened next, I had Savannah Burns to blame. Or thank.

...

All night, the temptation to delete my post grew. Through a series of techniques such as squeezing my nails into my palms, and tangling my legs in the blanket on the couch, I managed to resist until the gray glow of pre-dawn appeared. Then I snatched up my phone and turned it on. Time to weed out the blow-back from my TMI post and then drown myself in the reflecting pool of the National Mall.

As my phone came to life, notifications from Instagram spilled in. A lot of them.

My breath stopped in my throat—stopped absolutely short as if an elastic band had wrapped around my windpipe—as I scrolled through notifications. I had hundreds and hundreds of comments. Thousands of likes. Nothing I'd ever done had garnered so much attention. I checked Facebook, too, and it was the same, with hundreds of shares.

People had picked up the hashtag, too, making their own posts in their own voices.

Almost every inch of me wanted to cancel my accounts. Almost. There was a tiny, curious part, too, that wanted to know what was going on, exactly. How this had happened.

Hearts punctuated the responses. Messages from people I'd met, messages from strangers, all of them were supportive. Some of them, the people who knew me before, said they had no idea about my past. Some of them said they'd donated. I opened my computer for full screen access and checked my

GoFundMe account.

Holy shit. HOLY SHIT. I'd gone from $2,132 raised in a couple of months to $20,000 WITH ONE POST. I had to refresh the page to check whether it was correct, then run my fingers along the numbers to make sure I had the right number of zeros. Math hadn't been my strong suit in school, but I wasn't stupid. Savannah had promised to quadruple, but she had been wrong. She had fucking… multiplied the whole thing by ten in one night.

I let out a shuddering breath. This was amazing. How many bags of personal items did that mean for the kids? It had to be thousands. My mouth felt like it would explode off my face I was so excited. I stood and twirled around on the hardwood floor.

Hurriedly, I pulled on my skates and packed up my electronics in my bag. I had to tell Savannah, I had to thank her and tell her she was right, no matter how pushy she had been. Also a small part of me wanted to tell her she'd been wrong.

I made two quick stops on my way to see her. In that time, my excitement never dwindled. It had worked. I had been brave and it had worked.

Hadn't life proved to me again and again that when I was brave, good things came to me? Yet I was still scared, and Savannah had reminded me once again how important it was not to listen to fear. Not totally, anyway.

I knew so little about her except the location of her office, so I stopped there first. Since it was Sunday, only a security guard manned the lobby. I gave him a smiling wave as I skated through. He stared, but didn't question my entrance, finding his phone more entertaining than I was threatening. No one else was there, so I skated right through to Savannah's office.

She looked up from her desk. Her hair was in a loose loop at her neck and she wore no makeup to cover the bags under her eyes. In the second before her face changed, I noticed a new squareness to her jaw, as if she'd been clenching it all night long.

"Are you all right?" I said, breathless, panic pushing away the thrill of the earlier moments.

She smiled, though the smile didn't reach her eyes. "Just realizing the house I've built over the years is made of those little paper matchsticks."

There it was again. That sense Savannah wasn't as she seemed, like she carried something more than she revealed on first glance. The urge to make her feel better won over the panic. I placed a hand on my hips. "Is that all?"

Savannah choked out a little laugh, pulling the elastic from her hair and running her fingers through the loose strands.

"Is it work?" I asked, plopping down in the chair opposite her.

"No. Maybe?" She shook her head. "I'm so sorry. I shouldn't be complaining about... Wait a second. You're here."

Her voice brightened. I could practically see our last meeting playing through her mind. I wanted to start over, to do it all again. I opted for cutting the memory short instead.

"You were right," I said quickly.

Savannah quirked a brow.

I couldn't hold it in any longer. "You were right

about sharing my personal story."

"Oh yeah?"

"I did it last night and…" With shaking hands, I brought out my phone, tapping on the GoFundMe app. "Look."

Savannah burst from her chair, sending a whoop into the air. Her reaction tumbled from her like an exploding volcano I couldn't have stopped if I'd wanted to.

"I want to thank you," I said, standing and skating toward her.

She met me halfway around her desk and wrapped her arms around me, pressing her body up against mine. "Thank me for what? You did this. I knew you could do it."

Her fingers rested on the part of my spine where it met my neck, open above my shirt. The smell of coconuts surrounded me. My heart pounded against hers, my breath caught, hitched on a hook in my throat.

I hadn't been hugged in a long time. I'd been kissed. I'd been made love to, but not hugged. Why not? With her supportive words and the full length of her body pressed up against me it was as if my whole being short-circuited. All feeling stopped, and the urge to push away strengthened.

She let go first, and I managed to keep the smile on my face, though it probably didn't look real. Shakily, I moved around the desk, giving myself enough space to regain my composure and remember why I was there. Wow, this girl was really doing a number on me. Thank God I would be out of town tomorrow, or I would be in trouble.

"I can't believe it," I said. "All it took was one message."

If she recognized my awkwardness, Savannah didn't acknowledge it. "It must have been a strong message. How much more money did you make last night than usual?"

"A thousand times more than a normal night. Holy shit, the number is so huge."

Savannah sucked in a lip and glanced out her window. She folded her arms.

"What?"

She shrugged.

"You want to say something, say it."

She bit the inside of her lip, tapping her chin with one finger. I'd never seen her so nervous. "It can get bigger, you know. But I don't want to push you. God, I'm terrible at apologizing."

"Oh, was that an apology?"

"I'm sorry, ma'am."

My jaw dropped, the laugh spilling out of it. "*Ma'am*. Now you *really* owe me an apology."

Savannah cocked her elbows, a smile tugging on her pink lips. "It's mah southern upbringing. I'm so sorry *ma'am.*"

I'd come here to deliver my thanks and leave for a skate, though I'd hoped for more. Now, I couldn't imagine leaving without more. I couldn't imagine leaving at all. Once I'd laughed until my gut hurt, I stared at her.

"Thank you for seeing the best in me."

"It's not hard. You're… fucking… amazing," she said.

Fucking. She'd sworn, hesitating around the word

as if it needed a barrier from the rest of her speech. That tiny word was the hottest thing she'd done yet. "Come out with me."

Savannah glanced down at her desk, ran her fingers over the pieces of paper in a perfect stack. "I should stay."

"You should come."

"I've got so much to do."

"It's Sunday. The day of rest. Come rest."

"I can't." She lifted her narrow shoulder, a puny resistance if I ever saw one.

I skated forward and grabbed her hand. "We're going."

"No, I—" Savannah smiled a full smile, pulling out of my hand. "Okay, okay, just let me put on my shoes."

As she bent to slip on her shoes, I got a full view of her rear end. I turned around, my face heating. She could be a friend. That was all. A friend. Which meant no ass viewing, no kissing, no hand holding, and definitely no coveting.

I'd never understood the coveting thing. How could you stop yourself from thinking something?

Well, I was about to give it a try.

Chapter 10

SAVANNAH

I only pretended to fight. After the night with Lori, after I'd witnessed the structure of my relationship crumbling, after I'd found *no* solace at work where I'd usually found all my solace, I'd yearned for something to do. The fact Casey had shown up was like an answer to an unuttered prayer. And a path, perhaps, to rebuilding my foundation. Or to finding a new plan forward.

We traced E Capitol Street NE, through Lincoln Park, all the way to Anacostia Park near the river. It had been so long since I'd taken the time to just walk my city, and I had to admit, it was gorgeous, especially this time of year. The cherry blossoms were dazzling clouds of pink against the gray sky. The people seemed to be sensing spring as much as the plants, smiling, waving, joking.

As I walked, the deadlines and desperation fell away. There was a freedom here, right now, in this pause. Between projects. Between... girlfriends? Maybe.

Casey bobbed along on the bike path since the sidewalk was mostly brick, her skates a humming a tune, never faltering. Her small body taut and compact. A smile constantly on her face. She met me with a grin of true pleasure. My face stretched in a real smile, too. Had it only been the day before I'd thought she wasn't my type? What made me think that? Her beauty astounded me.

"Are you going to tell me where we're heading on our great adventure?" I asked once we'd reached the safety of the park.

In a burst of energy, Casey skated forward and twisted backward. She cocked her head, raising one foot and *still* skating backward. "I don't think so. That'll give you a chance to run."

"I'm not going *anywhere*," I said. It was one of those moments where the phrase held more meaning than I'd meant it to.

Casey turned again, hopping on her single foot and lowering her torso like it was a lever on the fulcrum of her thigh, until it looked like she was a dancer. No, better than a dancer. She was *flying*.

I ran to catch up to her, feelings crowding my chest. Feeling. It burst out of me in a string of words. "You're beautiful, you know."

"Stop it," Casey said, returning to a normal position most humans could sustain—both feet on the ground.

"I'm serious. There's a grace about you."

"About as much grace as an elephant."

"Some of the most graceful animals on the planet, if you ask me." I placed my hands on my hips and stopped.

Casey glanced back three times at my frozen form before rolling her eyes and doubling back. "What now?"

"Why can't you accept a compliment?"

Casey's eyes flickered, and I watched as she fought inwardly. It was the same the day I told her to share her story. Why had I pushed her *again*? It certainly wasn't going to help me get closer to her. I sighed, letting my hands drop. "I'm sorry, you don't have to answer. I'm doing it again. I'm being too pushy."

She lifted her chin, looking as regal as a queen. "I guess I just didn't receive compliments much as a kid and I still don't trust them."

It broke my heart to hear this, shattered it into a million pieces. I closed the distance between us, took her hand, and placed a kiss on her cheek.

Casey froze. "Don't," she said, closing her eyes.

"What? It didn't mean anything."

Her eyes opened, dark like a ripened blueberry. "You and I both know that isn't true."

"Of course it is." Even as I said the words I didn't believe them.

"You have a girlfriend. We have to… it's just… I can't do that, okay? I don't want to ruin anyone's life."

"My girlfriend and I—"

"Come on, we're almost there." Casey skated out of my grasp.

"We aren't doing well. Lori and me," I called to her back.

She shook her head. "It doesn't matter. You're still together. It would still be a lie."

She didn't wait for me. She rushed forward, swerving in an "s" from one side of the walk to the other. She crossed the street and stopped in the RFK stadium parking lot. When I finally caught her on my human feet, she knelt on the ground, working some bulging object out of her bag.

A skate. A matching skate to hers, except red. She freed the other. My stomach twisted in knots. "What are those for?"

"We're going to the park today."

"The what?" I said, the butterflies reaching full form.

"The skate park over there. I heard it was wonderful and wanted to check it out before I leave."

"When are you leaving?"

"Tomorrow."

I steeled my dropping heart in place. Of course she was leaving. She was only visiting, crashing on couches. She had no reason to stay. *Except me*, a small part of me wanted to say, but I couldn't say that. It wasn't true. Lori had me, technically.

Back to the present where I should be. Enjoying the moment. Though the moment wasn't all that enjoyable. Terror gripped my stomach like a vice, refusing to let go. Casey pulled at the laces, loosening them.

"My friend had an extra pair of skates she said I could have. She collects them and this is one of her old pairs. I thought I might see you today. Lift up your foot."

I kept my foot planted firmly on the ground, where it belonged, thank you very much. "How do you know they'll fit?"

"What are you, a size eight or so?"

"How did you know?"

"Good guess. Now, lift up your foot, would you, woman? Before I have to force you."

My mind scrambled for an excuse. It had been too many years since I'd skated. I would fall. I had no use for wheels. But deep inside that bass said, *yes*. It was time I start trusting that.

Casey peered up at me, kneeling. I placed a hand on her shoulder to steady myself and lifted my foot.

With tenderness, she slipped off my canvas sneaker then guided my foot into the skate. I watched as her fingers danced over the laces, tightening them and tying them together. That was the easy part, I still had one foot on the ground.

"Alrighty," Casey said, sliding the other skate nearer my left foot. She looked up at me. "Put as much of your weight as you need to on my shoulders. When I slide this other skate on, you're going to tuck the heel against the wheels of the other one, got it? That way you won't roll."

I felt like a little girl as I bit my lip. My hands braced on her muscled shoulders. She was so close to me, her head bending at a particularly inopportune place, the top of her ponytail poking against my thigh.

The skates, Savannah. Focus on the skates.

"How does it feel?" Casey asked, glancing up.

"Weird?" I said, cringing.

Casey laughed and started to rise.

"Whoa!" I kicked out one foot from under me and started to fly backward, until Casey caught me, her arms wrapped around mine.

"Don't freak out," she said. "It's not as hard as you think."

"You're just saying that because you've been skating forever."

"I'd never put on a pair of skates before this project."

I froze and for a moment, it felt like my feet were on solid ground. "Really?"

"Yeah, but the moment I did, I knew I never wanted to take them off."

And she hadn't. Barely ever. When was the last time I had followed one of my inclinations like that? Or even had any inclinations to follow, other than *work.*

"If I had followed my wishes like that, I may have ended up murdering someone."

"You wouldn't have."

My arms shook as they grew more tired of holding Casey's shoulders for dear life. "You don't know the people I work with."

Casey shrugged. "I've seen a lot of evil people and they're all miserable. Happy people don't want to hurt others. Hurt people hurt others."

I tilted my head. She was so *good.* I hadn't met anyone so good in so long. "You're amazing."

Casey smiled, a pretty blush coming over her face. I'd never seen her blush before. It was wonderful. "Do you trust me?" she asked.

I did. I hadn't trusted *anyone*, maybe since I was a kid, but I trusted Casey.

"I'm going to let go," she said.

I take it back. "No! Please."

"Put your feet in a V-shape," she said, her voice even and patient.

My weight totally on her, I did as she requested.

"Now, I'm going to let go and you're not going to move, okay? You trust me, right?"

"Yes."

"And if you don't trust me, trust physics. You're

not going anywhere when your wheels are bumping into one another."

I nodded. She was right, absolutely right. I was being a coward when all I had to do was close my eyes and let go.

...

CASEY

Savannah was a quick learner, though she was probably one of those people who was good at everything they decided to be good at. Within an hour, she was skating comfortably forward. So comfortably, I started to teach her to skate backward as well.

At one point, I found myself asking her if she was sure she'd never skated before. She laughed and reassured me the last time she skated she was six and clung to the wall the whole time.

"You're just a good teacher," she had said, and even that had sent my knees quaking.

The longer I spent with this woman, the more I got to know her idiosyncrasies, the more I was falling for her. She went after everything by attacking it. So, I shouldn't have been surprised she had mastered in one hour what it had taken me, and many others, weeks to learn.

It also shouldn't have surprised me when she pointed over at the skate park. "What do you say we try a ramp?"

"Really?" I searched her face for signs she was going to yell *just kidding*, or run away, or melt into a puddle or change into some humanoid alien carnivorous creature and devour me whole. Even that was a stronger possibility than this pretty girl wanting to stay and skate ramps with *me*. But that's what was happening.

I glanced over at the park, packed with the Sunday afternoon teenage crowd. "It's scary. The first time I dropped into a skate park I almost peed my pants."

"Let's go," she shouted, and started for the park, her red skates like flames on her feet. Going forward, she looked like she belonged here almost as much as anyone.

I scooped up my bag and skated after her. "Hold on there," I said, catching her by the arm. "If you're going in, you have to suit up. Pads, the helmet, the whole shebang."

"Won't that ruin the whole hot skater girl vibe I've got going on here?"

Her joke took me by surprise. Not that she never joked, but there was a lightness to it rather than a cutting edge. "Trust me, it's cool to wear pads in the park. And certainly cooler than sporting a neck brace for the next few months, or worse."

I got her suited up, trying to ignore the now light pressure of her fingers on my shoulders, the smell of her hair, the dimples that hadn't disappeared since I put those damn skates on her feet. That's what I'd wanted, right? To show her a good time? And she was having one. So why did I feel like this was going to end in disaster? "Now, only take on a little at a time, okay?"

"Okay, *Mom*."

"Seriously. It does not feel good to eat a mouthful of concrete."

"What, you don't like the taste? Too gritty for you?"

Another joke. Two. Another dance into this dangerous territory of temptation. I decided to brush it off with a joke of my own. "It's the missing teeth that bother me more. I'm so short people might mistake me for a kindergartner."

I backed away, surveying my results. Miraculously, she looked just as gorgeous in the elbow, knee, and wrist pads, as she ever had. Only Savannah Burns could do that. I handed her the helmet, but she pushed it back at me.

"I want to see you skate. Show me what you do."

I paused only a second before taking the helmet and belting it under my chin. The park had a series of rails, ramps, and steps. It was in decent condition, though not the best park I'd ever been to. I planned a course of action in my head, then started.

When I'm skating, the whole world falls away. I can't fret or worry or angst about the future or past, because I have to focus on what I'm doing. Distraction means injury. So as I skated over the smooth ramps, gaining speed, I forgot about everything. I hopped up on a rail and slid down. Then I bounced up some steps like a rabbit and gained speed down a ramp. I went up the next one and kicked up my legs, arching until I touched them, and landed with them back under me. The teens were watching. To show off, I jumped up on the next step and set off on a backward course around the park.

It was thrilling. I ended by doing a back walkover and skating backward to the place where

Savannah stood clapping, cheering, and whistling.

Still high from my skate, I slung into her arms, ignoring all the teens and preteens around me. She wasn't stable enough to hold my weight, so we both almost fell to the ground. Somehow, I managed to drag her upward until her body was once again pressed against mine in an awkward hug. Her feet slipped. She laughed and tried to reset them in the way I had taught her, still holding tight to my arms.

As my laugh calmed, we looked into one another's eyes, and I realized what I was doing was holding on. Too tight. What could come of holding on too tight?

Heartbreak.

Chapter 11

SAVANNAH

Every time I touched Casey, it was harder to let go. Every time, it added a log to the fire burning deep in my gut. I spent much of our time skating, when I wasn't intently focused on my task, arguing with myself. She was right. I was in a relationship. I barely knew Casey, and what did we have in common? Was I just going after her because she was different? Because I wanted the chase?

How would I ever learn to trust myself?

She let go first this time. I didn't let it get to me, though. I brightened. "Should I try going down one ramp?"

"Absolutely."

Casey led me through the crowd of teens over to the smallest shallowest ramp and taught me how to let my legs come up under me. Even this small ramp was scary, but when I did it, my stomach lurched in the best way possible and I squealed with glee. Actually *squealed*.

I started to understand why she never took off her skates. Rolling, even when you weren't going very fast, was addictive. When I told her this, she told me about the science behind it. How she'd watched a documentary that talked about how the inner ear goes into a sensory explosion when you skate.

"I want to try two ramps in a row," I said.

Anything to keep me from tackling her and pressing my smiling mouth to hers.

We waited for one of the teens to finish his skateboard trick on the ramp, then she showed me how to do the second, larger ramp.

I went down the first one. As I was approaching the second one, my mind clouded. Did I know how to stop once I got to the top? What would happen? Would I roll back down? Would I look like a fool in front of Casey?

By the time I got to the top of the second ramp, my stomach was in my throat. It was like I hadn't learned anything about skating. I tripped over absolutely nothing.

I slammed into the ground, my head bouncing off the concrete, and slid forward. Oh, God. Oh no. Did I break something?

Panic surged through me. What would I do with a broken leg or arm? Would I even feel it at first with all this adrenaline running through my body? Without breathing, I scanned my body for breaks.

A deep rumble of laughter started in my belly and burst through my mouth. I'd fallen and I was okay. The laugh shook my whole body and then Casey was kneeling by my side and I was looking at her through a half-dislodged contact, folded in laughter. Why was I laughing so hard?

"Are you okay?" Casey asked.

"Yeah," I said through a laugh, blinking the contact back into place. "I'm fine. I just…"

Casey let out her own skeptical laugh as she grabbed my shoulder. "Let me see your face."

I tried to calm as she turned me around and placed a finger under my chin. "Still perfect."

The laugh drowned in my chest. I had fallen and I hadn't died. I had taken a chance on something I would never have taken a chance on without her, and it had been okay. It had been better than okay. This was a sign.

I unclasped the helmet and set it on the ground, pulling my fingers through my hair to eliminate tangles. It was vain, I knew, but worth the reaction. Her eyes followed my movements. I drew my fingers across my lips. That hadn't been on purpose, but as her gaze followed them, the heat gathered and pulsed in my stomach.

She wore a gingham shirt, tied around her waist, showing a bit of her belly. Always with the belly. But now it wasn't her clothes was turning me on. It was the worry on her face.

I fisted her shirt in my hands and dragged her toward me. She hesitated, a battle going on behind her eyes. I crossed the distance for us both and kissed her once, keeping my eyes on hers. Her body melted forward, relenting. When I pulled away, she opened her eyes, and what I saw in them, I couldn't deny. They were so dark, almost purple, and so close to me.

She relented then, like the chains had fallen from her wrists, she drove toward me so hard, her lips pressing into mine so vigorously, I collapsed back onto my elbows. The pads saved me from pain.

Suddenly, the sun peeked through the clouds, warming my skin, illuminating shoots of red behind my eyes.

Fireworks. The fire consumed me. I wanted her more than anything I'd ever wanted in my life… but, not like this. I pulled away, still fisting Casey's gingham.

"I'm such an idiot," she whispered, her forehead on mine.

"No you're not." I touched her soft cheeks with my fingers, wishing they were mine—*all mine*.

"I shouldn't have done that."

"It's my fault."

"This—we can't."

"Yes we can."

"No."

"Yes, but not like this. I want to do this right," I said, pushing a pink strand of hair back against her hairline with my fingers. "You deserve more than a quick roll on a concrete park in front of a bunch of teen boys. You don't want to do that. You're good."

She clutched my wrist, just as she had when she'd written her number on my arm, and kissed my palm, sending a shiver through me. "You're good, too, Savannah, if you would just get out of your own way."

"You know what? I'm going to do just that. I'm going to go break up with Lori. Right now. I want to be able to give myself to you. All of me." As I said the words, I punctuated them with a clench of my fists at my sides.

After tonight, everything would be different.

Everything.

Chapter 12

SAVANNAH

Casey and I pored over my phone to find a decent hotel room—and I booked it for us to avoid any hassle. Then, reluctantly and after a long kiss goodbye, we set off in opposite directions, me for the Navy Yard and her for the hotel, calling promises to see one another soon.

Off to the *Navy* Yard to battle with my girlfriend. How fitting. Part of me just wanted to let it fade, or to do this thing with Casey without dissolving my relationship with Lori. But Casey deserved better than that. Lori deserved better than that, too. So, it was just going to have to happen.

I left my new skates outside the door. Then I took a breath and stepped inside.

Sunday was Lori's cleaning day, but when I entered the apartment, the dishes were still in the sink. I found her just as I had the day before—on the bed watching something on her laptop. Now I'd made my decision, I occupied this strange place where I could view her as both a stranger and someone dear to me.

"We need to talk," I said.

This time, she didn't try to put me off. She closed the laptop and set it down on the bedside table. She took her glasses off and did the same with them, rubbing the corners of her eyes. "I know. I have something to tell you, and you're not going to like it."

Though my brain knew whatever she had to tell me didn't matter, my stomach did a little flip. I edged toward her and sat on the bed.

"You go first," I said.

She bit her lip, shoving her fingers against it as if she couldn't get enough into her mouth. Then she moved to biting her fingernails. These nervous tics of hers had always annoyed me. They betrayed her true feelings, I'd told her, and you couldn't trust anyone with your true feelings. How stupid and hardened I'd been back then. All part of the game. This time, I let her experience them without judgment.

She stilled, dropping her hands from her mouth and meeting my eyes. "I've been sleeping with someone else."

My stomach fell out of my body, or that's what it felt like. Like dropping in an elevator, plunging toward my death. Disbelief ruled the following moments. "Who?"

"You don't know him. I met him—"

"Him?"

"Yes. Him."

I took a moment to process this. Him. Seriously? She was rejecting me for some bro dude on the Hill? For some no-doubt cocky penis-wielding dude on the Hill? My whole body shuddered at the thought, and I stood and crossed the room.

Lori, little mousy I-don't-care Lori, had an affair with a man.

A little voice told me to calm down, that I had essentially been having an affair as well, though I'd made this silly line and convinced myself I hadn't crossed it. It was the memory of Casey's lips on mine that brought me back to reality.

"I'm sorry," Lori said in a dull voice. "I felt stuck at work and stuck at home with you working so many hours…"

This was actually amazing. Not only could I be with Casey now, but I wasn't the bad guy.

"I didn't set out to have an affair," she said, her voice heavy with guilt. "It just happened."

Of course. I knew better than anyone, based on recent events, how these things could just happen. What were the chances I would go into the bathroom right when Casey had? Minuscule, but it happened, and the earth had tilted that day and remained tilted ever since.

When I turned around, I saw tears streaming down Lori's face. She wiped them away and sniffed.

"I want to honest with you, too." I took a step closer, the image of Lori with the Hill dude already fading. "I met someone as well. We didn't sleep together, but we've been talking. A lot."

Lori nodded, wiping the tears falling faster down her face. "How did we get like this?" she asked.

I perched on the edge of the bed. "It gets so easy to stay in a situation, even if it isn't good for you. I think both of us knew that, and both of us were too…"

"Stuck?"

"Yeah. We were stuck."

Lori's tears moved into sobs and I couldn't help but close the distance between us and wrap my arms around her. Her face was hot, her tears wet and her hair damp with sweat. I held her as she sobbed, mourning the loss of our relationship, something I'd already mourned a long time ago.

"We loved each other once, right?" she asked, pulling away.

"Yeah," I said, and it was true. We had loved each other, briefly, we just hadn't been right long term. I leaned forward and placed a kiss on her forehead. She pulled away and dried her tears and tried to offer me a smile. And that was it. It was over, in a way that was almost too easy.

"You can have the apartment," I said, moving back across the bed.

"Are you sure?"

"Yeah, I'll find a new place."

"And what about work?"

"What about it?"

"Can we still work together?"

I stared at Lori with her puffy eyes and blotchy cheeks. As I did, another feeling took hold. One of excitement, one of hope. I did all I could to suppress that, to be sincere with Lori. Here. Now. "If you're okay with it, I'm fine with it, too."

"I think I can do that." She sniffed. "God, this was much easier than I thought it would be."

There was nothing left to say. I rose to gather my stuff, but there was too much of it here, entwined with all her things. "Do you mind if I come back and pack later?"

"Not at all," Lori said.

Now the excitement flooded me, I couldn't hold it back. Tonight I was going to sleep in the arms of a woman who adored me, who cheered me, who admired me. Who I felt the same about. Tonight, the shackles would fall from my mind. No matter what happened, tonight I would have *fun*.

Chapter 13

CASEY

I stared at the doorway to the hotel room, waiting, waiting.

What had I done?

My only excuse was seeing her in the skates. The way she tackled learning them. The way she'd handled falling. It had been the way she'd laughed and the way her silky hair flew behind her, even under the helmet. It had been the way she kissed me, the fire in her eyes. It had all brought me to this place. This place where I was waiting for her to come to me.

What if she didn't come? What if Lori asked her back and she agreed? She had a history with the woman. Hell, she lived with her. I couldn't imagine being so close to someone and just breaking it off. I pushed off the bed and skated around the room.

Was I a bad person for kissing her in the first place? Had I caused this all to happen? Was I ruining her life by being here?

Shit. I hated waiting. I hated the in-between time. My mind got a hold of me, clawing at me like a tiger and squeezing my heart until I cried mercy.

Mercy. Mercy.

I was scared, and it made me want to run. But I wouldn't run, not this time. At least this time I could see it clearly. And I wouldn't let it take me over.

Sitting on the bed, I picked up my phone and scrolled through my contacts. Tomorrow, I was supposed to head to Alexandria, Virginia and crash with my one and only friend from home. Clari. I brought up her number and sent her a text.

I should be there tomorrow! Your offer for a room still stands?

After tonight, I didn't know if I could trust myself. This way, I would keep on my schedule, moving to Virginia this coming week and Maryland the week after. It was important to do that, to stick to something for once in my life. This challenge meant something. After the failed college attempts, the failed jobs, it was something I was good at. I wouldn't quit.

To pass the time, I thumbed through my social media pages and answered messages when I could.

A few minutes later, Clari texted me back.

If you're okay with me being a total mess and terrible company.

My stomach dropped. Clari wasn't given to hysterics. She'd been the most grounded girl in high school, which wasn't hard because high schoolers aren't exactly known for their levelheadedness, but still. While I was bouncing around from foster home to foster home, Clari was my pillar, my footing. Though we'd lost touch for years, she had gotten me through the hardest time in my life. If she was in trouble, I had to do something about it.

I called her, pressing the phone to my ear. It rang and rang until it went to voicemail. Switching to text, I wrote.

Are you okay? And a few minutes later. *What's going on, Clari? Do you want me to come now?*

As the minutes ticked by and I received no answer, my mind swirled. *Okay, be rational,* I thought, forcibly calming my quickening breath. If Clari was telling me she was a mess, she probably wasn't in danger, just hurt. Emotionally. But a mess could be physical, too. What if something happened to her and she wasn't telling me? What if she was trying to protect me?

She had always taken care of me, in a way. Maybe she was hiding something serious.

There was only one thing I could do. Stupidly, I still didn't have Savannah's cell number. She wouldn't be at work since she was with Lori. I couldn't wait for her here any longer. I pulled out my ratty spiral-bound notebook and ripped a page from the back.

I'm sorry. A friend is in trouble, and I have to go to her. I'll call you tomorrow. -Casey

I added my phone number to the note in case she wanted to call, then I swung the bag over my shoulder and busted out of there. At the desk, I found not the woman with steel gray hair with whom I'd checked in, but a younger man with a mustache watching a baseball game on a tiny television behind the desk. To get his attention, I rang the bell twice.

"Yes?" he said, his eyes never drifting from the screen.

"My name is Casey Day. I checked in an hour or so ago? Something came up. Are you listening?"

"Yeah, yeah, you checked in an hour ago. Go on. NO," he shouted at the television, not exactly inspiring confidence. What other option did I have?

I waited for him to settle down. "There's this woman coming here who will be looking for me. Savannah Burns. Can you give her this note?"

"Do I look like a carrier pigeon to you?"

My face flushed with heat. Is this how he was going to treat a paying customer? Part of me wanted to leave and forget about the note, but I couldn't do that. I had to make an effort, at least. I wasn't running from her, but to a friend. "I'm not asking you to bring it to her. I'm asking you to hand it to her when she comes to the desk. She should be here in a couple of hours."

The man peeled his eyes away from the screen long enough to look at me again, this time giving me the once-over. Apparently, I wasn't his type as his lips pulled up in a sneer, a barely there sneer he probably didn't notice. But in the end, he said, "Put it under the bell."

I picked up the pen on his desk, wrote Savannah's name in big capital scribbled letters, and stuck the corner under the bell. The man didn't bother to say goodbye as I left.

Okay, well then. He wasn't a decent human being, but I was. I was going to help a friend. It was the right thing to do in this situation. I couldn't help it if I failed to get a hold of Savannah before she reached the hotel. It would only be a wasted trip for her, where if Clari was really hurt I would regret not going more than anything.

This was the right thing.

So why did it feel so wrong?

Chapter 14

SAVANNAH

By the time I got to the hotel—a much smaller operation than I'd understood from the internet listing—my body was alive with promise. My fingertips tingled, sweet anticipation coated the back of my throat and pulled up on the corners of my mouth. I was *free*. Now, the only thing in my way were a few walls and a few layers of clothes.

As I entered the door of the hotel, I encountered a mustached man standing at the desk, his head bent under the ministrations of a stern older woman.

"How many times do I have to tell you to pay attention to what's going on here?" she asked.

"I was, Cin, I swear. Right here."

She put her hands on her hips. "At the TV screen, you mean. You can't have that at the desk. It's unprofessional."

"How about a radio? With headphones."

The woman tipped her head. "Will that help you pay attention?"

"I dunno."

"No. The answer is no. Now, go," she said, pointing out the door like she was talking to a misbehaving puppy.

The man hung his head, walking away with his mini TV from 1990 in his arms. She had displayed more patience than I ever could in a situation like that. I would have just fired him. Maybe there were extenuating circumstances. Maybe he was her son, or her husband in a strange twist of cougar-related events. If so, then power to you, woman.

Well, maybe not.

The woman grabbed an empty McDonald's wrapper from the counter and some scrap pieces of paper cut into shapes, as well as some loose paper. She threw it all in the trash, muttering to herself the whole time. No matter what, she didn't deserve cleaning up after a guy like that. No woman did.

As she straightened up, my mind turned back to Casey. I could imagine her strong body slung out on the bed like a lounging cat, her hair down and wavy. Those damn skates still on her feet, dangling. Totally open to me. It was a dream, just like skating arm-in-arm the first time I'd daydreamed about us, but hadn't that come true? Or close to it? This one was so close I could taste it. Taste her.

Just thinking about it thinned my patience. I had already waited so long. I didn't want to wait any longer. "Did a Casey Day check in here earlier?" I asked.

The woman frowned.

I'd stopped at the grocery store for some food and other items and picked up Sushi on my way here. I shifted the bag of groceries to my other arm. "She had pink hair. Skates, probably."

The woman's face brightened. "Oh yes, I checked her in myself. The room was under the name… Burns?"

"That's me." Though I knew I wasn't doing anything wrong, my face flushed with heat. I'd never done anything like this before. Meeting a congressman in a hotel, sure. Not that we ever had sex or did anything like that, though some probably expected it. But a woman? With whom I was about to have consensual, legal sex? Unhindered by other relationships? That's what I was embarrassed about?

Maybe some therapy was in order here.

"Room 395. Here's the key." The woman handed me a key card. I thanked her, gathered my stuff, and left, taking the elevator up to the third floor. At the door, I slid my key into the lock. I opened the door, a smile creeping over my face.

"I'm here," I said.

No one answered.

The bed cover was rumpled, but Casey definitely wasn't in it, nude or otherwise. I set down my groceries and checked in the bathroom. No Casey there. Maybe she'd gone out on some errands, but if that was the case, why didn't she leave a note or something? Anything. Why hadn't I given her my phone number?

I settled on the bed to wait, turning on the TV and flipping through the stations. But as I flipped, my mind began to wander. I'd seen something in her face as I left her. Fear? But she'd promised she'd stay. She promised she wouldn't leave me here. Had she?

The TV just added noise to my rambling thoughts, so I turned it off and watched the red digits of the digital clock on the bedside table tick by.

Maybe she left because she realized I wasn't good enough for her. There was that night at the party when I'd been so drunk. And I had put moves on her when I was with someone else.

Ugh, this was getting ridiculous. She had to have left word somewhere. Maybe at the front desk. I made my way there.

"Excuse me."

The woman looked up.

"I was wondering if Casey—the woman with pink hair—checked out or if she left word here or something? She's not in the room."

"You know," the woman said, picking up a key card. "I was wondering who this card belonged to. Maybe she did check out. Leon's not the best at noting these things down. Let me see if I can scan the card... and..." Her eyes moved on the screen. "Yep. This was for room 395. She must have gone."

"Odd," I said, still not freaking out. Not yet, though a dam held back stormy waters filled with feelings. "Did she leave a note or anything?"

"I don't see anything here, do you?"

I scanned the desk. "Maybe Leon knows. Maybe she said something to him."

"I'd ask him, but he's out for the night, and once he's out for the night, he won't respond to anyone or anything with more than a groan. Trust me."

The playful side of my mind didn't analyze this comment any, it was overtaken by worry. She had left her card here, and... What? Had something happened? Was she okay? It was late now, dark on the streets. I didn't like to think about her skating through D.C. at night when she didn't know the area all that well. It wasn't a bad neighborhood, but you had to be careful.

"Did you try calling her?" the woman asked.

"Thanks for help," I said, unable to speak about

Casey any longer. I turned away.

I'd never been much of a worrier. If something happened, I was always able to take care of it by getting another news appearance, or by convincing one of the representatives to take a deal with a well-placed bit of information. Or by finding out what they didn't want me to know and exploiting that. There was always something I could do.

Not now. With Casey, there was nothing. I knew her, in a way I didn't even know my own parents. I knew she was open and kind and joyous and forgiving and thank goodness for the last one. But I didn't know anything concrete about her. I didn't know her family or her address or even her phone number, which I regretted more than anything else now. The ink on my arm had long ago faded, unlike my attraction to her.

I pulled out my phone and navigated to her social media account, but I found nothing there after the heartfelt post from the day before and a few replies from earlier. Well, at least I knew she was okay at 5:36 PM, but two hours had passed since then. Two hours was a lot of time to get in trouble. I sent her a quick private message, but I wasn't connected with her on social media, so I doubted she would get it.

My throat dried. What if she was in a hospital room somewhere right now? Or worse, a morgue?

She could take care of herself, another side of my brain argued. But that would mean she'd just left— and I didn't think she would do that.

I had to approach this like I would any problem, step by step. And the first step was looking at the last place I'd known her to be. She wasn't there, I was almost sure of it, but I couldn't overlook anything. Hopefully, I wouldn't have to get to the next step—the hospitals.

Hopefully, she was just out. Hopefully she'd dropped her key and someone had brought it back to the desk. Hopefully, I wouldn't end tonight in tears rather than in ecstasy.

Chapter 15

CASEY

The Uber ride to Alexandria depleted more of my funds than I would have liked. Due to an accident on the Washington Memorial Parkway, I didn't arrive at Clari's until past what was decent for visitors. I didn't care. I pounded on her door.

She didn't answer, and the door was locked. During my ride, as Clari kept not answering me, my worry had increased. I tried to keep it cool, but I didn't have many long-term friends in this world, and I couldn't afford to lose this one. Sure, I hadn't seen or spoken to her for a while, but that didn't matter.

When she didn't answer within a minute, I pounded on the door again and rang the bell. There was noise from inside, then the door clicked open on a bleary eyed Clari, her dark hair knotted on one side. She squinted, then her eyes flashed open.

"Are you okay? Get in here?" She pulled me inside. "I thought you weren't supposed to arrive until tomorrow."

"I thought you—are you okay?"

"Yeah, I'm fine. Just sleepy." Her eyebrow shot up.

It was then I noticed the state of her apartment. Boxes lined the wall. Her shelves were empty. Her artwork leaning against the tables and chairs rather than on the wall. "You said you were a mess."

"Yeah. Look around." She gestured into her apartment. Her apartment was a mess, or as close to a mess as Clari would ever get. She was not a mess.

"Why didn't you text me back?" I said, dropping my bag to the floor. I'd removed my skates in case I needed to deal with a situation when I got there. Though Clari said she was fine, my eyes searched the dark corners of the room and the open doorways for someone menacing. I turned back to her. "I was worried about you."

"I must have fallen asleep." She folded her arms over her T-shirt clad chest. "Do you want something? Some water… or?"

I blinked. I'd been riding so high in the last hour, now I was cresting for the crashing plunge. My eyelids grew heavy. I looked back at Clari. "You're fine."

Clari cocked her head.

I broke away from staring and made my way to her couch.

Clari dashed ahead and pulled a painting out from under me as I sank down. I was barely aware of her movements. Like I was watching a television show from the corner of my eye, I could only see the broad strokes. She sat on the opposite side of the couch with her legs tucked under her. Far away. So much space. Had I created this space?

"How long has it been?" I asked.

"Too long," she said. "And I'm sorry we can't have more time before I move."

I hadn't even known she'd been moving. How out of the loop was I? "Where are you going?"

"Portland."

"The Maine Portland?"

"The Oregon Portland. Back to the left coast."

"Oh." I stared down at my hands. Clari and I *had* been good friends at one point, hadn't we? Or had I just made it up?

"What's wrong?" she asked.

The words were like warm water on my skin. Calming. *I* could control this, I could control whether we would get closer in this moment or further away. I could reboot this relationship. And I wanted to. I wanted someone I could call, someone who would get up in the middle of the night for me.

And I needed to figure out this mess I'd made with Savannah.

I played with my fingers in my lap. Fidgeting. "I think I might have done something stupid."

"Really? You?"

I glanced up at her to find a smirk on her face. Leaning forward, I swatted at her. *This* was why we'd been friends. What had made us lose touch? Time? It didn't matter now.

"I met a woman," I said.

"Another notch in the—"

"She's different."

"Gosh, you could have let me finish the joke at least. Skate. Another notch in the skate. Har har?"

I bit my lips and raised my eyebrows, giving her a good glare. She was wearing gym shorts with an oversized T-shirt. This woman had legs for days and long naturally wavy deep chestnut hair. I'd never felt anything for Clari, not like that. She was straight, anyway, and I'd had enough trouble in my life without falling in love with my straight friend. "Not even a little bit funny."

"Wow, you really did meet a woman. One who made you serious. That's impressive."

"I've never felt this way about someone. We haven't even *slept* together, but she makes me feel… like I don't have any edges. You know what I mean?"

"Not really."

I shrugged, unable to describe it. "She makes me feel like I want to stay."

"You say that like it's a bad thing."

"It's terrifying. I've finally found something meaningful to do with my life—"

"Great job on that, by the way." Clari put her hand between us.

Heat rose to my cheeks. "Thanks. And the thought of giving it all up doesn't sit well with me."

Clari nodded, processing what I had just told her. "Why would you have to give it up?"

"Because I can't continue traveling *and* have a healthy relationship."

"Can't you?"

"I don't know. She's a challenge."

"And how do you feel about that?" Clari pulled down her hair, letting it fall over one shoulder. After high school graduation, our paths had gone separate ways. I had tried and failed to get through three community colleges, and she had gone on to do an accelerated master's program in social work. I'd thought we'd have little in common after that—no, I'd made *sure* we'd have little in common.

Imagine if I could have gone through the last six years with this kind of conversation. Maybe I wouldn't be so damn messed up.

I blew out a breath. "Conflicted, honestly. We were supposed to meet at a hotel tonight. I had to leave her to come here."

Clari paused for so long I thought she may have dropped off in the middle of the conversation, but when I glanced at her the assumption flew right out the window. She glared at me with her wet clay-colored eyes. "You didn't have to leave."

"Yeah, I did. I thought you were—"

"You left because you were scared."

I put up my hand. "Listen, I already know that's a flaw of mine. I run away because of my childhood and now I do it whenever I'm scared, blah, blah, blah. It's boring even to me so I'm not going to go on about it, but, this wasn't it. I thought you were in trouble. You're important to me."

Clari put her hand over mine. "And you're important to me too, which is why I'm telling you to go back to that hotel. Right now."

My body resisted the suggestion like it was a foreign object, breaking out in a cold sweat, soaking the underarms of my jean jacket. Just the thought made me want to stand up and scream. I couldn't go back. I couldn't. "Isn't it kind of late for that?"

"Never."

"I left a note with my number for her. She'll call when she gets it."

"Yet she hasn't called."

"I really should figure out a cheaper way to get back to D.C."

"I'll spot you some money."

A clock made its presence known by ticking in the silence. With each tick, a boulder set on each of my limbs. Suddenly, I received a flash of myself panicking as if I was outside my body. "What would I say to her?"

"The truth?"

I couldn't show Savannah how dumb I'd been. Seriously, who would text her estranged friend if she was in trouble rather than call the police? It was like the part of my brain responsible for common sense shut off whenever I was about to get into a truly intimate relationship. Though I had come here, *toward* an intimate relationship. Progress, right?

"Do you have her number?"

"No, I never thought of asking for it." Another evasion tactic of the anti-intimacy part of me. I stood, pacing to the edge of the room.

"What about calling the hotel? What was the name?"

I rattled off the name and the location of the hotel and Clari looked up its phone number on her laptop. She gave me the number. I called, and a woman answered.

"Hi—this is Casey Day. I'm looking for—"

"Savannah."

"Yes," my heart lifted at just the sound of her name. I was such a fool. "Can you put me through to her room?"

"Sure. No problem. Hold please."

I danced as the woman put me on hold and transferred me to the room. It rang and rang and rang and with every ring, my heart sunk into the quagmire again. She wasn't there. I hung up and called back.

"She's not answering."

"Maybe she stepped out?"

"It's important."

"Do you want me to knock?"

"Yes, please."

Clari met my eyes as I waited again for the woman—who was much more helpful than the man I had encountered at the desk earlier in the evening —to see if Sav was there. I turned away from Clari's hopeful eyes. If this ended in disappointment, I couldn't take hers, too.

The woman returned.

"Ms. Day? I'm sorry, she's not there, but if I do see her I'll tell her you called. Want to leave your number just in case?"

I did and hung up the phone. When I turned back to Clari, my chest was full enough to burst. "I promised her I'd stay. If she thinks I left…"

"Why don't you get some sleep? You can call her at work in the morning and tell her everything you wanted to say."

I nodded. I would be more rational in the morning, and better able figure out if I had fucked up the only good thing that had happened to me in a long time.

Chapter 16

SAVANNAH

When I returned to the hotel at five the next morning, after searching all the hospitals and morgues, the woman at the desk told me Casey had called and she was all right. My body practically gave out under the pressure of the night. Unable to do more than get to our room, I collapsed on the bed and fell into a deep, dreamless sleep.

I woke to a buzzing vibration next to my head.

I picked up the phone to see a text from Lori. *Where are you?*

It took me a moment to understand why she was asking the question. Had I just dreamed of our breakup? But then I realized, thanks to my phone, it was Monday. And it was ten in the morning. And we were supposed to meet the new client at ten.

Still in my Sunday jeans, I was nowhere near presentable for a client meeting. I texted Lori back, telling her I was running late and would be in before eleven. She sent an angry emoji, but I wasn't sure what I could do. The apartment and work were in separate parts of the city, and I had already used my spare outfit after the night of the party.

It took precisely forty-five minutes to get back to the Navy Yard, change, grab my things and get to work. I arrived, groggy, and popped a couple of pick-me-ups. It struck me then I hadn't taken any of those pills during my time with Casey. A whole weekend without them. I couldn't remember the last time that had happened. They were becoming a daily part of my routine—like brushing my teeth or washing my face. I would have to get rid of them some time. But not today. Not when I was late and I needed to be on. I popped another for good measure and pushed through the glass door of the main office building.

Lori caught me at the entrance to our office and dragged me inside, closing the door behind us. "What the hell, Sav? I know we're both going through something right now, but late for a meeting? That's not like you."

"I lost track of time," I said, setting my bag down next to my desk.

"You've lost track of your mind, apparently."

"You're perfectly capable of running a meeting, Lori. You could give them the numbers point of view, anyway." I blinked. Maybe not. "Are they still here?"

"Yes, but they want you. You're the superstar."

I wasn't feeling like a superstar. I was feeling more like dog turd. "Do we have coffee around this morning?"

"Sav." Lori stomped over to me and grabbed my shoulders. "What is going on with you? Are you… what's wrong with your eyes?"

"I didn't get any sleep last night," I said, stumbling backward, averting my gaze.

"I can cover for you, if you want. Tell them—"

"Absolutely not. Just get me some coffee. Please." I started to leave the room.

As I left, I thought I heard Lori say something

about being a fool, but the good thing about exhaustion was I could easily ignore her. So I did, continuing toward the conference room, where hopefully I could still win over our client. My limbs were starting to shake, in the way that meant they had an excess of energy rather than a lack of it. Show time. I arrived at the conference room just as a group of three men in suits were leaving.

"Gentlemen," I said, settling into my normal self. Feeling a little invincible, if one could feel just a little invincible. "I'm so sorry I'm late. Please, sit, I won't take up more of your time than I need to."

They looked at me like I was wearing the head of an elephant, but I was reasonably sure I still had my head on my shoulders. I gave them a smile, knowing the dimples would tame any lion in the room. And they did. It worked. The men walked back to their seats.

"You must be the famous Savannah Burns," one of them said.

"Indeed." I braced my hands on the table. "And I am going to make sure we get this law passed so we can stop losing good people."

It didn't pass over my head that this was kind of ironic, based on what I'd taken earlier. The difference was I didn't have a problem. I could stop any time. I'd had an off night and needed a boost to get the job done. Plus, it wasn't like I had slid down the slippery slope into heroin or cocaine. I hadn't made it to *Wolf of Wall Street* status or anything like that.

"Lay it out for us, Savannah," the same man that had spoken said. "How can we win this thing?"

"Personal stories," I said. I remembered how well

it had worked for Casey, and every time in the past. At the memory of her, a twinge of worry flicked my stomach. *Steady, Sav. She's fine.* I put on my smile again, like a sun hat at a garden party. "People love stories, right? They spend their time watching TV, reading books, lost in other worlds."

"But isn't that for escape?" the spokesman said.

"Sometimes, yes. But ultimately people are looking for truth and connection."

The men looked at one another, unconvinced. Or at least that's what their eyebrows said.

"I don't just mean slapping a sob story up on TV. We don't want to make people feel hopeless, though we do want them to see the extent of the problem. The law can be the hero of the story. We just need to explain how."

Sometime in the past few moments, Lori had stepped into the doorway. She tapped me on the shoulder and handed me a mug of coffee. Tim had slipped in behind her, too. This was it. This was my performance evaluation. I'd already jeopardized it by being late, I couldn't fail now. I had to close this deal. Everyone was counting on me.

"I come from Louisiana, from a family of educators. College professors. High school teachers. I was kind of an oopsie baby, thirteen years younger than my older brother, and they all spoiled me rotten. When I was seven, my brother overdosed. My mother found him in his room. He didn't leave a note, he didn't mean to die. No one could save him."

The people around the table, including Lori and Tim were dumbfounded, their mouths practically hanging off their chins.

"You know what could have saved him?" I said. "Narcan."

My eyes filled with tears, but just because I think I'd forgotten to blink. Not because I felt something for the story. I couldn't feel a thing but a blast of energy. "Your law would require paramedics to carry Narcan and if that was the case, my brother would still be alive today."

The men seemed aghast, not sure what to say. I was, too. I'd never told this story to anyone. Not my friends growing up, not even Lori, whose face was a shade of pale I'd never seen before. The sadness in the room was palpable and was growing heavier by the moment, but I knew how to read a room.

"See how you're feeling now? Sad for me. Right? What if I then showed you a version of the story where someone was saved? You'd feel hopeful, right? That's how I want millions of people to feel around the country. I want them to feel that and then pick up their phones and call their representatives."

The men looked at each other, silently nodded.

"And that's just a story I made up off the top of my head. Imagine if the story was actually true," I added.

The men blinked. I had done my job, so I sat in silence, letting the story settle. "We're in," the ringleader finally said.

I felt nothing. My insides were all blasting at the same volume, the same tone. Merry-Go-Round, clown, carnival music. My own horror movie soundtrack. My stomach roiled, rancid with my story and the exhaustion, laced with the pills I'd taken. I remained as long as I had to close the deal, then left.

Lori chased after me, "Sav, are you all right?"

"I need a few minutes, okay?" I entered our office and closed the door, leaning up against it.

A few seconds later, my phone beeped. I crossed the distance to my desk and pressed the intercom button.

"There's a call for you. Casey? On line one."

"Thank you. I'll take it from here." *She's alive and calling.* I took a breath, trying to shake the music, trying to turn it down. I picked up the phone. "Are you all right?"

"Yeah, I'm fine. A friend had an emergency and I had to go. You didn't get my note?"

"No," I said, deflating into my chair. "Where are you now?"

"Alexandria."

She hadn't been killed or kidnapped or any other horrible things I'd imagined as I was looking for her the night before. Wired from my meeting, my brain tripped over this information. "Is your friend okay?"

"She's fine. It's—I need to talk to you in person. Will you meet me tonight?"

I dropped my head, pressing my fingers into my eyes, my arm holding the weight my neck couldn't. I wanted to. I wanted to more than anything, but last night had left me ragged as a torn flag in the wind. If we were going to do this, I would have to set my boundaries. For the job.

But I wanted to. "Where?" I asked.

"Vermillion, in Alexandria?"

"See you at eight," I said and hung up.

My energy was already starting to fade and my

day had barely begun. If I wanted to get through my work day and go to dinner tonight, I would need an extra boost. I would need more than my body could produce on its own.

Chapter 17

CASEY

Only a few times in my life had I ever been as scared as I was waiting for Savannah at the restaurant. Those other times had been much worse than this—life changing, and not in a good way. What was I so worried about now?

I'd borrowed a dress from Clari, a dress with a plunging neckline showing bits of my heart tattoo. I'd slicked back my hair so it didn't look so hot pink. I'd borrowed a pair of shoes, too, ones that pinched my little toe. All for Sav.

In the time I'd spent with Clari, I'd discovered something. We—Sav and I—had been going about this all wrong. Backward. Tonight, I would start at the beginning and move forward.

Sav arrived wearing a sleek black dress and two-inch pumps. It was a simple ensemble, but it accentuated her tall body and her perfect curves. She looked like a classic movie star. Maybe it was also my nerves, but she looked taller than usual, too. Almost domineering. I could see why she was good at her job—not that I had seen her in action, but I knew it from just looking at her. As she scanned the room, I stood, my legs quaking. I gave her a little wave.

More serious than I'd ever seen her—which was saying something since she was often pretty serious —she made her way to the table.

She was about to break up with me, if one could break up with someone they weren't even with. I knew it as soon as I looked at her and she didn't meet my eyes. My strategy shifted.

I couldn't lose her. Not now. Not when I'd finally decided to commit. I licked my lips and tried on a smile, gesturing for her to sit down.

"How was your ride?" I asked, inwardly cringing at the stupidity of my comment. "You look beautiful."

"Thanks." Her eyes slid down to the menu, then back up at me through her lashes.

Okay, maybe she wasn't breaking up with me. Maybe I could breathe. *Breathe.* Except I couldn't breathe because I was really doing this. All of it.

"I ran."

"Hm?" She flipped the page of the menu.

"That's how I cope when I'm afraid."

Savannah set down her menu, braiding her fingers together. "What are you afraid of?"

You? A relationship? Life? Every single move I make? I broke away from her searching gaze. "I don't even really know. I think… some deep part of me knows if I don't stick around, if I don't make lasting relationships, I can't be disappointed."

Savannah sucked in her lips and nodded. There was a vibration about her today, a high energy flick to her movements, though she wasn't fidgeting. Someone like her wouldn't fidget, but her eyes lacked focus.

"Are you feeling okay?"

"Yeah, I just downed one of those 5-hour energy drinks. Didn't get much sleep last night looking for you."

Her words held no accusation, but they hit me like a blow to the gut. "I can't believe you didn't get my note."

"Where did you leave it?"

"At the front desk. With the dude with the mustache."

"Leon." Sav rolled her eyes and let out an exasperated sigh. "We can blame him."

I still hadn't told her all of it. All the gory details. She had to know what she was getting into.

"I apparently will make up just about any excuse to run—last night, it was my friend Clari, but she was fine. My foster homes as a kid weren't even *bad*, you know? But they weren't good, either. I just wanted to be with my mother… even if that wasn't possible."

Sav stretched a hand across the table, covering mine. "Do you like anything on this menu?"

Had she heard anything I just said? I was pouring my heart out to her, and all she could think about was food?

Before I had a chance to question her further, a slow smile spread across her face. "It seems a little hoity-toity to me. What you say we go somewhere fun?"

My senses couldn't quite compute what she was saying. It took me almost a full minute to understand that her hand on mine, the smile on her face, even her question was saying *I see you. I hear you. We don't need to talk about this. Come, be with me.*

I could only give her a nod. That's all I could risk

without letting the tears fall. Her hand tightened on mine and she pulled me up from my seat, practically dragging me out of the restaurant.

I hadn't realized the upscale restaurant had made me jumpy, but it had. As we hopped into Sav's rental car, the jitters fell away. We rode with the windows open, the wind whipping our hair.

"This is the best idea you've ever had," I yelled over the howl of the wind.

Sav turned her megawatt smile onto me, her curls separating and blowing everywhere. "Want some pizza?"

"I thought you'd never ask."

We stopped at the next pizza chain and took a box to go. We drove until we found a dirt pull-off at the top of a hill. We parked, then we leaned back our seats ate our pizza with the twinkling stars as a backdrop. Rarely had I been in a situation where somebody expected nothing of me. Where I didn't have to perform or didn't have to be on. But here I was. I could just be me. She knew the worst. She knew I'd run, and she'd decided to stay.

I learned a few things while eating. She snorted when she laughed really hard and ran her fingers along the tops of her thighs when she was nervous. She even did some killer impressions, including Marilyn Monroe, which was helped along by her superstar face.

I found myself angling toward her, fully on my side, as if I wanted my whole body to experience her. My fingers, my breasts, my thighs, my face—none of it wanted to miss a second.

We'd settled into a silence, Sav gazing up at the

sky, me enthralled by her. She opened her mouth to speak, then closed it. Then opened it again. "I grew up with a mother and father, but I know what it feels like to be ignored."

I wasn't sure what to do or say. For me, she had freed me by not dwelling in the story. That was the best thing for me. What was the best thing for her? Would she like to talk about it? Or was this her way of acknowledging what I'd said earlier? Of relating? Only one way to find out.

"Oh yeah?" I asked.

Sav tried to smile, but it fell fallow on her lips. She met my gaze. "My brother died when I was little."

My breathing grew shallow, as if drawing in a full breath would drown out her voice. "I'm sorry."

"Overdose. I barely knew him. He was thirteen years older than me, another adult in my life. But after he died, it was like my parents went with him. They could barely function. They never really cared about what I did after that, they only cared about the child they lost."

"They couldn't see the wonderful child they had. That's horrible."

Sav shrugged, a little gesture meant to convey a sense that she'd gotten over it. Maybe for the first time in my life, I recognized someone else's pain. That was a shitty thing about having a terrible childhood. It shorted my empathy. Something I was only realizing now. That, and it made me judgmental of others when they didn't deserve it. If Sav had never forgotten her clutch, I never would have gotten to know her because of that judgment. To think.

I crawled over the center console and straddled her waist. Holding her chin in my hands, I placed my lips on hers. "I want to stay here. With you. To be with you."

Sav brought her whole body to meet mine. Her lips, her abdomen, her breasts.

The heat kicked up a notch as my hands pulled at her zipper on the back of her dress. Sav froze. She gathered my hands in hers. She pulled her face away from me, set her forehead on my hands. "Wait."

Terror wrapped its tentacles around my heart before releasing. "What is it?"

"I want to do this right."

"I do, too. That's what I meant for tonight to be all about."

Sav rolled her forehead along my palms. "I'll be distracted in the next couple of weeks trying to pass this drug bill. I need my focus. My promotion depends on it."

"I understand," I said pulling my leg out from where it was trapped between the seat in the door.

"No," Sav said. "I mean, yes, of course I need to focus on the work, but I want to focus on you, too. All my relationships before this have just kind of happened. I don't want to be like that with you. I want to do everything with intention. Do you know what I mean?"

"Yes," I said, though I wasn't entirely sure what she was saying. My brain was still too tingly with her lips and her hands all over my back.

"A few weeks. Can we wait a few weeks until sex?"

"Absolutely. Sure."

"I hear anticipation makes everything better."

I laid my head down on her chest and listened to her heart beat in rhythm with mine. She wrapped her arms around me.

I would wait for you forever if I had to.

That thought, and the feeling of home I had in her arms, were absolutely fucking terrifying.

...

"Talk me down."

Clari sat cross-legged on the floor surrounded by boxes. I'd forgotten how expressive she was, and while her colorful things were packed away, she brought her own color and sound to a room. Calm now. Like the shushing of ocean waves. "Do you want me to talk you down?"

Yes. No. Sav I had spent the night in her rental car. Talking, laughing, making out like teenagers who hadn't yet lost their virginity, and sleeping in one another's arms.

While with her, I was totally sure of what we'd agreed to. But time—even the few hours since we'd parted—eroded my certainty, like a tide biting away at the shore. What right did I have to *want* and *enter* a relationship? Did I even know what a romantic relationship involved beyond sex?

Skating all day until my legs wobbled didn't help, though I had some nice road rash on my arm from a failed trick. It always helped, but not now. And why? So, we'd decided to get serious. You'd think I'd be relieved. It had even been my goal for the night. But that was the thing with me, I could want one thing one second and it would become my worst nightmare the next. A process I couldn't seem to control.

"She said she wants to focus on me. Only me. They call her The Closer. Isn't that kind of terrifying?"

"I think it's sweet," Clari said with a shrug.

"But you're moving across the country for love, so I don't want your opinion."

"Then why are you here?"

"Because we're only on the same coast for a few more hours, and I wanted to see you." *To make up for lost time*, I added in my head. *To cement our friendship before separating again.* I would keep in touch this time. Now I'd opened up the intimacy door again, I needed it.

Clari smacked her lips in disapproval. She had talked me off many a ledge, but this time she was talking me *on* to the ledge. Off the ledge, on the ledge, either way I was jumping. "What if she commits to me and then finds me boring?"

She's not going to find you boring," Clari said, her voice going flat. "If anything, she'll find your excitement exhausting."

"Am I really exhausting?"

Clari leaned forward and took my shoulders in her hands. "Listen. If you keep looking for reasons to run, you'll find them. That's how it works. Look for reasons to stay."

She had a point. The more problems I looked for, the more I would find. But I couldn't just let myself screw it up, and I knew if left to my own devices I would do just that. I sighed, flopping on my back, staring up at her popcorn ceiling. "I don't know if it's worth it. I was happy before I met her."

"Were you truly happy if meeting someone throws you off so easily?"

God, Clari. I turned my head and narrowed my gaze at her.

She didn't seem fazed. "I guess the question is… Will you be happy now if you leave? Will you be able to live with that?"

That was, indeed, the question. Could I just stay on the road after having met her and pretend like none of it happened? I squeezed my eyes shut. This is why I hated relationships. They create fissures in the road that turned into potholes, then sinkholes I couldn't cross. "How do normal people do it?"

Clari took a long time before answering, as if she were picking the words from a pile of Scrabble letters.

"Normal people," she said, emphasizing the normal, "have as much trouble as you troubled youth do."

She leaned forward and pinched my nose. I swatted her away. "Seriously."

"Seriously." Clari widened her eyes and nodded once. "People who were brought up with two parents may have had a good example of how it was done, but sweetheart, no one's perfect. My parents fucked up all the time."

Fuck up was not my memory of them. They were the couple I put on a pedestal. "But they were wonderful and so in love with each other."

Clari picked at the tape on the box next to her. "My dad has a terribly moody side he never showed in front of guests. He snaps at my mother all the time. I hate it. And I tend to do that, too, like I inherited it from him."

"And Paul puts up with that crap?" I asked, miraculously conjuring up the name of her boyfriend even though my mind was still stuck on Clari's parents. If they had trouble, how the heck could the rest of us survive?

Clari shrugged. "He makes me want to be better. And I have, kind of. I've trained myself out of the habit of snapping so much."

"I can't wait to meet this guy. He sounds great."

Clari didn't let me get away with my attempt to change the subject. She leaned forward and took my hand. "Does Savannah make you want to be a better person?"

"Aren't I perfect already?" I asked, waggling my eyebrows.

"Sure, perfect as that box you wrapped over there."

"I wanted to make sure no one could break into it."

"I won't ever see my mugs again."

"You can thank me when they arrive at your destination unbroken."

"Casey."

"Clarissa."

She wouldn't let go of my hand. If I let her, she would miss her plane holding my hand. She was stubborn like that.

I tsked. "Yes, and she already has made me better. But how do I know she won't—"

"Nothing is a guarantee," Clari said cutting me off. "You could die tomorrow."

"I know," I said, trying to pull my hand away.

"That's why I live my life like every day is my last."

"It's the same with love. You can't predict it, you just have to take what you can get."

Clari held my hand for seconds longer than I was comfortable with, but the longer she did the more her words sunk in. They both scared me and electrified me. I lived with uncertainty in my daily life. Hell, I didn't even know where I was staying the next week, so why did I push it away when it came to love?

"Who will I have to talk me down when you're gone?"

Finally, Clari pulled her hand away. "It's called a phone. Use it."

I laughed, leaning against a box and staring into Clari's face, trying to memorize her so the next time I panicked like this I could imagine her talking me down. Maybe that would be enough.

A ringing phone interrupted my next thought. I didn't recognize the number, but I didn't recognize many numbers coming into my phone. I answered.

"Is this Casey Day?" a deep voice said on the other line.

"Yes, who's this?"

"I'm a producer with *The Sally Sullivan Show.* Do you have a moment to talk?"

"Who's this really? Jonathan? Eric?" They were a couple of prankster cowboys I'd met on my way through Texas. They must have seen my viral post and were pulling my leg now.

"No, my name is Chris Hold."

"Okay."

"I see you're creator of #mywordsmatter."

"Yes."

"Sally would like you to come on the show."

Thump. Thump. Thump. My heart beat lurched. The house was silent, the clock that had ticked packed away now. Clari's eyes were open wide, and she gestured with her hand in a question.

"Hello?" the man asked.

"She wants… me? To come on the show? What do I have to share?"

"It sounds like you have an interesting story based on your post. And what you're doing really is inspiring to so many people. Did you hear there was a new hashtag too? #CaseyRocks?"

"Now you're *really* yanking my chain."

"I'm serious as a heart attack."

Thump. Thump-thump. It felt like both my hearts were beating, the real one, and the image of the one on my chest. Heart attack. Attacking hearts. "When?" I said, my throat scratchy.

"We tape next week."

"Can I get back to you?"

"Yes, but make it no later than tomorrow. I'll send along some background questions to your email. Nice speaking with you, Ms. Day, looking forward to hearing from you."

I dropped my phone.

My brain ticked forward waiting for the response from my body. Waiting for me to say *hell no* and run. But that wasn't my first response. My first response was something else. "I can't believe I was so stupid."

"What?" Clari asked. "What happened?"

"Sally Sullivan wants to interview me."

"Sally… what?"

"Right?"

Sally Sullivan. Millions of people watched her show every week. "Do you know who I want to tell most?"

"Who?"

"Savannah." As I said her name, I dialed her number, the smile on my face spreading wider. I was on the cliff, ready to leap. I just hoped Sav was there to catch me.

Chapter 18

SAVANNAH

One night of sleep in the front seat of a rented Camry, tangled in the arms of a sensual woman, did not a rested Savannah make. Still, the cloud of boredom following me around, even during the winning moments of my biggest successes, had dissipated.

In a former life, not too long ago, I would have stayed at the office later and used this energy for good, but I had made a date with Casey that night and I wasn't about to blow her off. I'd ruined one relationship that way and wouldn't make the same mistake again.

The Grand Hyatt Hotel was sleek and modern, all beige and browns. I arrived at the lobby, avoiding the staff so I wouldn't have to speak. The elevator carried me up to the fifth floor. As I dug for my key in my purse, a voice startled me.

"Well, hello there, beautiful."

The little hairs on my neck stood as I froze, an image of Casey flashing in my head. Until I gazed at her. She was more alive, more smiling, more colorful than my memory. She held a bouquet. My heartbeat picked up its rhythm. She was mine, mine, mine, it sang. Officially mine.

I eliminated the distance between us and she received me with open arms, moaning a little as she sucked in a breath. "You smell nice."

"Are you sure that's not the flowers you're smelling?"

"Nope, it's you," she said, and placed a kiss on my neck right below my ear. A shudder radiated from that point, like a drop of water in a pool. Gosh, resisting her would be difficult. Difficult, but necessary.

I pulled away and resumed digging in my purse. "I thought we were going to meet in the park."

"I wanted to surprise you. I brought flowers to brighten up your room."

I paused my search and pushed my face into the flowers. Tulips and daffodils. Oh, they smelled sweet and earthy, heady. They smelled how I was beginning to feel in Casey's presence. I kept my gaze on my purse, afraid of what I would find in her eyes. "They're gorgeous. Where did you get them?"

"I borrowed them."

"From where?" I asked, a smile playing on my lips, unable to resist looking at her any longer. Not that I had tried for long.

"From the park."

"And you're going to... return them when we're done?"

"Okay," she said, shimmying her shoulders in a shrug, "so maybe I didn't borrow them. But they have plenty. I made sure to scatter the ones I took. No one will even notice."

"You," I said, finding the key and pulling it out. "Are incorrigible."

"You and your million-dollar words and you—whoa—check out these digs." Her face went slack as she took in the suite.

The room was as sleek as the lobby, cream and glass with eggplant colored accents and fat-cushioned couches. The flat screen television took up almost an entire wall. The room looked almost as expensive as it was. "I figured I should treat myself since I'm working such long hours. You're welcome to stay if you want. There's plenty of room."

"I, uh…" Casey's entire face pinked as she let out an awkward laugh.

Why had I asked her *that*? Wasn't it just repeating my prior relationships? Rush, rush, rush. "You don't have to if you don't want to. Just if you *need* a place, you know, you can—"

"Shut up." Casey took one step, setting down the flowers on the table, and ran her finger down the side of my face. "What do you say we make good use of the room?"

"I say we had a plan."

"Of course, of course, but there are a lot of things to do other than sex, you know."

I didn't know if I could resist her. Everything about her oozed sex. Her low, husky whisper, the way her hips pressed into mine. *Think, Savannah, think. With your head.* "Hey, you know what?" I said, breaking away. "Congratulations are in order. You're going to be on *The Sally Sullivan Show*. Are you nervous?"

Casey sucked in her lips, raising her fingers to them. Nervous habit. "Naw," she said.

"Bull puckey."

"You and your crazy swears."

"I swear."

"Like a good southern belle," she sang with a twang.

"It's just not proper or necessary."

"See?"

She was about to reach out, I could see it in her movements. She was about to come toward me again and kiss me and I had to avoid it. "You must be nervous. Let's practice."

Casey groaned like a teenager who didn't want to take out the trash, turning away from me and moving to the fat couch. She plopped down on the cushion. "We have plenty of time. The interview isn't for a couple of weeks."

"The time will fly by, and you need to practice every day to get comfortable."

"It's so gorgeous out today. It's such a waste of good weather."

I moved, putting the glass table between us, my hand on my hip. "Sally Sullivan is a tough cookie. You don't want to flop on her show."

"You think I'll flop?" Casey's voice cracked on the last word.

"Of course not, but you need to practice. Ten minutes today, then we can go out."

"Fine." Casey punched her fists into the couch, then flopped over. "This fabric feels like a cloud on my cheeks."

Well, she was already an expert at deflection, so we could use that aspect of her personality for good. It was the posture we would have to work on, the body language.

"Sit up straight."

"Yes, ma'am." Casey bolted upright.

"First lesson," I said, ignoring her playful grin. "Don't let your emotions control you."

"Deploy robot mode, got it."

I turned and paced along the edge of the table. "If it helps you to think like that, it could work, but not too much. You want people to see your pain."

"I was *joking*, Savannah."

"I know, but this is serious. Sally Sullivan is the queen of making people crumble on stage."

"Geez, thanks for the reassurance."

"This is not about reassurance. It's about preparation. I've prepared a half-dozen people for that show, and the ones who didn't listen to me walked off that set shaking after the earthquake that was Sally Sullivan. You need to keep your focus, okay?"

"Yeah." A tiny crease appeared between Casey's eyes. She pulled her shoulders back. The smile was gone.

Good. Now we could really get to work. "I'm going to ask you a couple of questions, just to see where we stand, okay?"

Casey didn't answer vocally. When I glanced up, her eyes were on mine. Ready.

"Why were you in foster care?"

"My parents died," she said, her face melting into the emotion. *Good for viewers.* She kept her posture and her hands still.

"How?" I asked.

Her shoulders slumped forward. "My father died in a motorcycle accident when I was young. My mother died in a fire."

"That's horrible," I said, but quashed the urge to

cross the distance to her. I wouldn't be able to console her onstage. She needed to be able to manage her emotions on her own.

"Yeah, sure."

"What was it like in foster care?"

"Shitty, but not—"

"Now, you don't want to swear because this is network television and they'll have to bleep you out. Plus, it'll make you seem…"

"Uncultured?" she asked, peering out from under the pink strands of her bangs.

"Well?" I said.

Casey sagged into the couch, the cushions dwarfing her. I took a step toward her, then reminded myself this was helping her. It was practice. Sally would be much worse.

"Let's try this again. What was foster care like?"

"Difficult, of course."

"Specific, Casey, you want to give specific details so people will empathize with your story."

She sat up again, shaking her head. "I can't speak for all kids, but my experience was lonely. Extremely lonely."

"Good."

Casey's blue eyes hardened, a shell I hadn't seen on her. To be honest, a shell I'd expected to see on her, after what she'd been through. A dull, blank stare.

I turned away. "You know what I mean. And what were your foster parents like?"

"Is this how you treat your clients?"

"Yes, and they thank me for it later."

Casey fisted her hands, digging them into the

couch. "Can't we just talk about Voices for Love? What I'm doing now? Why do we have to focus on the past?"

Casey was both my girlfriend, and someone who was consulting my professional advice. That meant I had an *in* I didn't have with most of the people I prepped. I knew her story. I knew how she reacted when she was afraid. I couldn't treat Casey like another one of my clients because she wasn't.

I edged my way along the coffee table and sat down beside her, taking her hand. "You're doing what most people do which is identifying with your past, reliving it every time you tell it."

"How else can I tell my story?"

I turned to her. "Something I've learned to do is to see my past as something that happened to another person, another Savannah."

"How?"

"Well, how do you feel when you're Pink?"

A smile pulled at the edges of her mouth. "Like a capable queen."

"That's because your past didn't happen to Pink. It happened to Casey. So, what if you pretend you're Pink? And you tell your story as someone who cares very deeply for Casey but *isn't* Casey."

Casey's hand tightened on mine. "That could work."

I held on for a moment longer before squeezing her hand and standing, walking to the other side of the table once again, taking on my Sally persona. "Ms. Day, what were your foster parents like?"

Casey glanced out the window of my hotel room and took in a breath. Her hands didn't move. She shrugged. "I had a really nice family when I was young, but they couldn't keep me because they had their own issues. After that, I went to a family who ignored me. And that's when I started running."

"I'm so sorry for that," I said, still being Sally.

"Was that better?" Casey asked.

"Yeah," I said in a breathy tone, my voice vanished.

"Give me some more, baby. Bring it on."

My chest tumbled emotion like a clothes dryer. Why had fate put her through all this? She was so strong, so beautiful.

And I would never be good enough for her.

Chapter 18a

CASEY

I'd never been so busy in my life.

Maybe if I had gone to a four-year college, I would have understood how to juggle work and homework and clubs and friends and classes, but I'd never had that experience. I'd worked hard, McDonald's for a few years then retail, but it had always been on someone else's schedule. I could always come home and crash. Now, dealing with my newfound social media fame, juggling contacts with blogs, keeping up my skating schedule, and practicing for *The Sally Sullivan Show* with Sav, was running me ragged.

This was more an observation than a complaint. I was in contact with the director at Voices for Love, and we had come up with a new program for all the funds I was earning. She even hinted there may be a position open for me at the organization when I was done.

I couldn't have done it all without Sav. She had given me a key that unlocked the chest to my heart. I would never have thought that distancing myself from my story would have worked, but it did. It was helping me talk about it in a new way, and each time I did, it hurt a little less. I was able to dig a little deeper, to find a little more.

Plus, it gave me something to do other than

envision Sav naked in bed with me. A couple more weeks until we could let it all go.

One day, Sav called to cancel our date, saying she had a client who was panicking at a local television station. I was already on my way, so I asked if I could join. Just to watch. Sav agreed.

By the time I got to the station, it was dark. I made my way inside, asked where I could find Savannah Burns. Without a word, the person at the desk led me to a conference room. Savannah waved me inside as soon as she saw me.

The woman at the table was surprisingly young. At first, I thought she was twelve, she looked too thin and small to be much older. But when I got closer, her face showed signs of someone older. Maybe eighteen or twenty. I swallowed down my shock and stuck out my hand.

"I'm Casey," I said, "but you can call me Pink if you want."

"Sam," the girl said, giving me a limp shake. She made fleeting eye contact with me before taking her hand away and crossing her arms again, staring at the table.

"Casey is experienced in this sort of thing," Sav said.

The girl didn't respond. She was listless, at best. Not what I would expect from someone panicking or from someone Savannah had prepped. If Sav thought she wasn't stable enough to go on TV, she never would have put her in that position.

"If by this sort of thing you mean torture at the hands of Savannah, then absolutely."

The girl didn't answer, but her mouth flickered at

the corner. I glanced at Savannah who opened her eyes and shook her head, giving a little shrug. She looked at about wit's end, and by the stances between the two, I imagined it wasn't going all that well.

I placed a hand on my chest. *Mind if I give it a try?*

Sav gestured to the girl.

I took the seat next to her.

"You don't have to do this if you don't want to."

"I want to," the girl said.

"Why?"

"What do you mean?"

"Why would you do this if you didn't have to?"

Her eyes moved back and forth across the table, then locked on mine. "Because I want to help other girls."

"By going on TV? Why not… opening a door for someone? Or, baking cookies. People like cookies."

"Cookies won't help girls with Moms who are addicts."

I sucked my lips in. "No, but this law could, right? It could help them get the care they needed?"

The girl nodded. She seemed weighed down, like she carried a bag of sand on her shoulders.

"You know what? Let's get up," I said, bouncing to a standing position.

The girl glanced up at me, squinting as if I was too bright for her.

"Come on, come on. You too, Sav."

Savannah stood, her eyebrow perched high.

"Hands up high in the air like you've just scored a goal. Stretch, stretch, stretch. There you go."

The girl tentatively put her arms up in the air.

"Higher. Spread your stance a little. How does that feel?"

"Kind of stupid." Sam glanced down at her body.

"Embrace the stupid. Now do a jumping jack."

The girl did a jumping jack. Then another without prompting.

"Why are you doing this?" I asked.

"So other people don't feel so damn lonely."

"That's it," I said, surprised at the girl's increased vigor. A smile pulled at her lips.

"Touch your nose with one finger," I said.

She did.

"Hop on the opposite foot."

She did, then stumbled to the side and laughed. It was like the movement had broken something open inside of her, releasing a waterfall of laughs.

"You don't have to do this," I said as the laugh died down. "There are other people who can do this."

"I want to. My mom's depending on me."

I sucked in my lips to stop a sudden hotspot of emotion blooming in my chest from pouring out of my mouth.

"Excellent, then let's get going. The producers are probably out of their minds," Sav said, moving around the table and guiding Sam out of the room. As she passed me, she stopped. "Why don't you go freshen up, Sam? I'll be right there."

Sam agreed and closed the door behind her. Sav's eyes moved between mine. "You're amazing."

"You did most of the work. I just came in and got her moving again."

"I don't think I could have gotten her back on

board."

"Aw, shucks."

"Seriously." Savannah took my face in her hands and kissed me, sweet and long. When she pulled away, she had a smile on her face. "You're ready. You're ready for whatever comes next."

I didn't need her to tell me that. I knew I was ready, but her comment broke something inside of me, too. It threatened to spill over the emotion I had been successfully holding back.

"Get out there," I said, giving her ass a good whack. "Before I make a wicked woman out of you."

She pressed her body up against mine. "And what if I said I didn't care?"

"I didn't make the rules, baby."

Her face was an inch away from mine. I could smell a sweetness on her breath, as if she had just eaten one of the cinnamon buns from the café where we'd met many Saturdays ago. My body beat with hers. But Sav had to work. So I did the responsible thing, breaking our hold on the moment. I heard her open the door, but it didn't close again.

"I think I'm falling in love with you," she said.

"I—"

The door closed.

And she was gone, leaving me alone with my beating heart and sweating palms, and a driving need that was growing bigger by the day.

Chapter 19

SAVANNAH

The next weeks were anything but easy. My days were filled with terrified pharmaceutical companies, battling and lashing out like animals in the final throes of death. I was working fourteen and sixteen-hour days, trying to find people to tell their stories, reading and scouring multiple sources for ideas or hints of anything rumbling under the surface. All the while, the ghosts of my past remained out of view. I didn't go looking for them, either.

What made it tolerable was, at the end of the day, I got to see Casey. She remained in the D.C. Metro area, hitting the surrounding states in an arc. I rented a car to go wherever she was. All the while our impending separation dogged me. If she kept on doing what she was doing, we wouldn't have much time left. It would get progressively harder as she moved farther away from me.

I didn't forget about our plan. I thought about our eventual sexual rendezvous more than any other single subject other than work, imagining Casey's body as it bent and contorted, her strong muscles firing. But the vote was coming up soon, too.

Needless to say, I wasn't getting much sleep. Somehow, I'd been doing it all, staying on top of it like I was Queen of the Hill. Until we rolled into the last week of May.

That week, the pharmaceutical companies went on full attack. They took the stories I had gathered, the exposés I'd managed to get into the hands of important media contacts, and started debunking them with "facts." If the people I interviewed had a past, they found it. They were playing dirty. And I was aggravated.

One evening, after a particularly harrowing phone call in which I had to talk down one of my clients who the drug companies had exposed, jeopardizing his job, it got to be a little too much. I was going to have to work almost all day to fix this, and I didn't know if I would get to see Casey that night. Her interview with Sally Sullivan was the next day. I had hoped to get in a last practice round before the taping.

My eyes were growing heavy, and I didn't know if I would make it through my workload, never mind an evening with her. Not for the first time lately, I reached for my pick-me-ups, opened the pill bottle, and popped a couple into my mouth.

Sugar rush.

"I'm on my way home. Do you need anything before I leave?" Lori said from the door.

A flash of terror ran through me as I opened my drawer, threw my pill canister inside, and slammed it shut.

Way to go, Sav. You really pulled one over on her there.

"Headache?" she asked.

Only after a second did I glance up to see Lori's eyes staring at me. I could read her like an open book, and now her pages said *I'm worried about you.*

Was she suspicious of me?

I had to shut it down. "Iron. The long hours are wearing me out. I'm just going to stay here a couple more hours to see if I can run any more damage control."

Lori didn't move. I wasn't looking at her, but I could still see her from the corner of my eye, her suit a blur of brown tweed. I could still hear her breathing. Sense her eyes boring into the crown of my head. "You should get some sleep tonight," she said.

"I will. Of course I will." I picked up a stack of papers and tapped them on the desk to straighten them.

"You'll be much fresher in the morning if you do."

"I know." I pushed away the annoyance that crept into my throat and threatened to spill into my voice. Lori didn't have a say in how I ran my life any longer, if she ever had. "Why are you worried about how I'm sleeping now?"

"You seem… tired."

"I'm fine."

I apparently didn't say the words with enough conviction because she remained in the doorway, staring. "I know. You think I'm stupid, but I know."

She didn't know a damn thing about me. "Really, I have to get back to work now, Lori."

"Those things aren't good for you," she said. "You'll crash and burn eventually."

"Good thing I only need to get through the next week, then."

Lori swallowed and for once in her goddamned

life, she wasn't backing away. For years, she sat on the sidelines and watched our relationship fizzle, but the one time I needed her to back off, she wouldn't. "You have a problem," she said.

My phone rang, and I checked the caller ID to see my mother's number again. My parents had been calling for the past couple of days, ever since the battle with the pharmaceutical companies had publicly ramped up. My mother had even left me a message checking on me, which was an odd thing. Since when did she care enough to check on me? I turned over my phone, and the ringer went silent. If only I could do the same with Lori.

"The only problem I have right now is you're talking to me when I'm supposed to be working."

"Hiding behind your work again, Sav, you'd think you would have learned."

"I'm not—"

"Whatever."

I shouldn't have answered this. I should've just shut my mouth and sat, ignoring her like I would a fruit fly. A surge of energy ran through me instead. My vision narrowed, pinpointed. "Are you jealous?"

"Jealous? Are you listening to yourself?"

"Just go away and mind your own business, okay Lori? Just because we share an office doesn't mean we have to actually talk."

Lori's face turned red. "Suit yourself. Just because we broke up doesn't mean I stopped caring about you, you know if you need anything…"

"I'm fine," I said, probably a little too emphatically. My pick-me-up was in full swing and I needed to take advantage of it while I still had time.

Lori left, and once again I was alone at the office.

Was she right? Did I have a problem? I could stop anytime. It just wasn't an option that minute. Just then I had to finish my work and then be there for the woman who I was quickly falling in love with. I had to be superwoman if only for a short time.

Then I would quit and leave it all behind.

You know what? I could quit. I could quit right now.

I opened my drawer and reached in, pulled out my little tin, and stormed to the bathroom. The pellets fell into the toilet and I flushed, watching them spin away.

Problem solved.

Chapter 20

CASEY

"It must have taken you a lot to get past the situation, to dedicate your life to these kids. May I just say," the reporter leaned forward and touched my knee. I did my best not to flinch. "On a personal level, Casey, I'm amazed by what you've done. I know our viewers will be, too."

I could just imagine the ticker tape running across the bottom of the screen with 1-800-IDonate. I quashed down my apprehension and remembered what the exposure could do for the cause. The studio lights glared down at me, but by this point in the interview, I was used to it. Barely sweating, even.

Sally Sullivan was a tough sparring mate, but she wasn't as tough as Sav. While she asked hard questions, they were framed in pity. Her helmet of bottle blonde hair and full face of makeup made it easy to pretend she was just a robot, though. A robot with pearls. And Botox.

"Can I ask you a question?" I asked, challenging both myself and her.

"Shoot," Sally said, as if she had heard the word from her grandkids and was trying it out to seem cool. It wasn't working.

"If I weren't a foster kid, would you ask the same thing?"

"That's a good question." Sally shifted in her

armchair. "To be honest, I'm not sure of the answer."

"Most of society expects us to fit certain labels. Troublemakers. Users. Abusers. Runaways. Nobody expects us to do anything great, so why would we ever rise to an occasion that was never presented to us? It's a failure of imagination."

"I never thought of it like that," Sally said, tilting her head.

Win. "Exactly, that's why I wrote that post. It's important we raise our expectations for these kids, while at the same time providing them the resources to meet these expectations. I'm just one person, I can't speak for all the foster kids in the nation, but doesn't everyone just want to be treated equally?"

Sally nodded and started wrapping up the interview. I somehow managed to remember to tell her where to find the contact information for the Voices for Love. I managed to remember to smile, to shake her hand, and not fidget as the camera swiveled and zoomed on her.

She gave a closing statement, the director called it a wrap, and I shook hands with everyone on set. With each step, my elation grew, a balloon swelling in my chest, pushing at the edges of my mouth until I could do nothing but smile. Energy coursed through my limbs as my gaze swept over the small crowd for Savannah. I couldn't immediately find her. I also couldn't go searching for her at the moment, as the producers wanted to give me a final rundown of how the video would air. Right in the middle of talking to them, I noticed Savannah come from backstage. She stopped, scanning the film set. She looked tired. Even more tired than when I had met her. As soon as her gaze met mine, the exhaustion vanished.

Her face broke into a wide smile, dimples and all, and she crossed the distance to me, wrapped her arms around me and lifted me into the air. She squealed and I let myself echo the squeal. She put me down and pulled away, keeping hold of both my hands within hers. "You rocked it."

"Really?"

"Really. I couldn't have done it better myself. We practiced all that together, and I still felt compelled by your answers. By you."

My chest flushed with heat. I'd worn the dress I borrowed from Clari when we'd gone on that date, Savannah and me. It suited me. I wouldn't necessarily have bought it for myself, but it worked when I needed to dress up for an occasion. Plus, it was good luck. It reminded me of the night Savannah and I decided to do this for real. Since then, my life had been a dream. A dream beyond imagining.

"I couldn't have done it without you," I said.

"Sure you could have. It was in you all along."

"Wow, I'm dating a fortune cookie now. How lucky am I?"

Savannah punched my shoulder. "Next time, you'll do even better. And the time after that, and the time after that, until you're more of a pro at this than I am."

My heart beat quickened at just the thought. "Next time?"

"After that showing? All the news outlets are going to be after you. You'll probably need a publicist soon."

The thought of all this absolutely terrified me. But so far, I'd been terrified at every step and I was still okay. As long as I stuck to Savannah's advice, I was fine. Everything was going so damn well, but I could feel myself waiting for the crash.

As I was mulling this over, Savannah pulled her phone out of her pocket and checked it. "Lori's been calling me all day."

"Your ex?"

"Yeah, but not about our relationship. About work. Hold on, let me just check."

Savannah noodled around on her phone with her finger. The joy and excitement and adrenaline were still running through me so I hopped a little to avoid exploding.

In the meantime, Savannah frowned, paled. I didn't think her face could tell any more, but it could. It grew a horrible shade of green like the night of the party. This time, I wouldn't leave her alone in a cab.

"What's wrong?" I asked.

"Nothing." Savannah's eyes flicked up to mine, then back at her phone, then back at me. She shook her head and slid the phone in her pocketbook. "Nothing."

"Savannah, what is it?"

"It's nothing, really." Her words grew softer and softer as she stared into the distance, her fingers running over her lips, her opposite hand clutching her elbow. She looked as if she had witnessed a train crash.

"Is something wrong with your parents? With

Lori? With the vote?"

Savannah shook her head harder as if she was trying to shake out whatever she had seen. "You want to celebrate? Maybe get a drink?"

She sounded like Savannah. If I closed my eyes, I wouldn't know anything was wrong. But as she forced herself to look at me, I could see it. Paleness around her chin. The dimples a distant memory, though she still smiled.

She checked her phone again.

"If you don't tell me what's wrong…" Before I finished my sentence, I snatched the phone away from her hands. There was a YouTube video there, a video of someone talking in an interview setting, like the one I had just endured.

Savannah tried to pluck her phone from my hands, but I ripped it away and pressed play. My skates have given me the ability to dodge and dash and move quickly enough that nobody could catch me, even when I was on my feet rather than the skates. It worked well for the next minute as I watched the video.

At first, I didn't understand what I was seeing. It was a man, probably about thirty, with a strong southern accent. He was talking about Savannah Burns, about how she came from a family of drug abusers. About how she was using her clients for her own gain, exploiting them, while protecting her own family.

The words ran through my head, and still I couldn't quite understand them. Her brother had overdosed. Why would that be a bad thing? Why would that work against Savannah's cause?

It didn't matter now. All that mattered was the horrified look on Savannah's face. This wouldn't just go away with a joke. I had to dig deeper. Be there for her, like she had been there for me.

I slung my arm around her shoulder and hugged her close. "Let's go back to your hotel okay? We'll figure it out. Everything is going to be okay. It's all gonna be okay."

Chapter 20a

SAVANNAH

During my time in D.C., the number of ways I learned to destroy someone had grown tenfold.

For the insecure, it was as simple as expressing disappointment. Or scowling at them in the parking lot. For the stronger, threats helped. There were other ways, too. Psychological ways. That was the worst—the nuclear option—and exactly the type of war the pharmaceutical companies were waging on me.

They'd brought out everyone I'd ever wronged and put them in the spotlight. It was a constant barrage of the Many Ways Savannah Burns Sucked.

I got it.

But I wasn't going to take this without lashing back. I was going to find out who was behind all this, and when I did, I would make them pay. I just had to figure out how, and until then I would ignore the calls from Tim and Lori. This was my battle and I was going to have to find a way to win alone. I didn't need to dirty anyone else's hands.

"Why don't you sit down for a minute?"

The voice shuddered my thoughts to a halt like it had applied the parking brake.

Right, I'm in a hotel room with Casey. Oh God, Casey.

I squeezed my eyes and shook my head and sat

down on the bed next to her. "I'm so sorry. We should be celebrating."

"I understand," Casey said. She surprised me and placed a hand on mine. It was a surprise not because I thought she was incapable of feeling, but because I didn't know she could do this part. This hard part. She was still here, sitting next to me, her hand on mine.

"Hitting back at them won't work, you know."

Had I said that out loud? Or had Casey just been able to read my mind? I started to protest, to say I wasn't planning on hitting back, but it wasn't true.

"I want them to feel like this, too," I said.

"I know, baby." She slid her arm over my shoulder and leaned her head on mine. "You know what you have to do, right?"

My brain was a muddled mess of anger, of grief, of replaying the clip in my mind a hundred times. Had my parents seen it? I hadn't heard anything from them yet, not since the videos started. I pulled away from Casey's head slightly, so I could look at her. "Murder's looking awful good right now."

She didn't laugh. Not even a flicker of a smile. "You have to tell your story."

I was already shaking my head before the words had completely fallen from her mouth. "It's not about me. It's never about me in this job."

"But it *is* about you now. It might suck, but this video makes it about you, and you have to respond to that, you know?"

Even now when Casey was trying to be serious, she had a lightness about her. A bouncing joy. I felt the opposite—like someone had poked a hole in me and all my blood and energy were dripping out. "I don't think I can do that."

"I thought the same thing." Casey took my hand, shaking the mattress as she turned to me. "But you made me see it was the right thing to do. This is the right thing for you too. If you stand back, get some perspective you'll—"

I ripped my hand away. "Please don't try to tell me how to do my job." I was lucky I had inserted the please in there as otherwise the viper would have gotten a full bite of Casey's flesh. As it was, it had grazed her. I closed my eyes, struggling to put the monster back in its cage. This wasn't good. I needed to think.

I stood from the bed, separating myself from Casey.

Something had happened at her interview earlier in the day. While I had been in the bathroom, I met one of the producers. Well, met is a strong word. Really, I'd caught her snorting a line of cocaine at the sink. She had barely acted surprised. I had surprised myself, however, by asking her where she got it, and if I could buy some off her. I walked out of there with a little baggie in my bra. That baggie was still there. All I had to do was go to the bathroom and take a little hit and I would be able to think again. I would have some clarity after a jumbled day without my pick-me-ups. I wouldn't have this exhaustion running through me, dragging me down.

My fingers practically twitched with need.

But I could feel Casey in the background, staring into my back. Waiting for me to calm down. To explain. To fix myself.

I could be good, like her. For all the flouting of the rules, she had the strictest set of morals of anyone I'd ever met. And they were good morals. The kind that could make you a good person. I could do that.

My need was almost insurmountable, driving my legs forward as if someone had a remote control and was making me walk toward the bathroom.

Instead, I managed to redirect to my luggage. Using my blazer as a shield, I put the little baggie in my suitcase, took off my blazer, and threw it on top.

There.

The first step wasn't the hardest. Every step was, adding a new set of chains to the load I carried. As I approached the bed, Casey opened her arms. I crawled into them, collapsing into her, hoping she could hold me there. Hoping she could keep me from spiraling down into that dark place.

I snuggled my face into the space between her chin and her chest, my cheek resting on the heart on her skin. Smelling her scent of mint. Feeling her long, slow breaths. Watching the tiny ricochets of her chest as her heart beat. She held me close, squeezing me to her.

It wasn't enough. The urges shot through me like lightning flashes. *Do the drugs. Figure this out*. My body was so damn tired, but my brain was on fire. I lifted my face. Casey stared down at me. She had taken off her makeup from the interview, and I could see now she did have this conventional beauty about her. Blonde under all the pink. Freckles under all the foundation. She could make me forget. She was the only one who could make me stay present in the moment.

I lifted my lips to hers and shimmied up the length of her body, placing a kiss on her mouth, my full weight on her. A moan vibrated through my lips, but it hadn't come from me. It was her. It started my engine. My hands went searching under her shirt, over her smooth skin, until it met the rise of her breast.

She pulled away, her eyes hooded. "I swear, Sav, if you touch me like that, I'm not going to be able to wait any longer."

"I don't want to wait."

"But—"

I cut her off with a kiss that showed her I meant business. Didn't I always mean business? Wasn't I always serious? I straddled her, unzipped my dress, and pulled it over my head.

Casey watched in horror. Partially to stop that look on her face and partially to stop the thoughts in my head, I grabbed her shirt and pulled her up, our lips meeting halfway in a kiss. Casey leaned away. "Are you sure?"

"Yes, I'm sure," I said, going back to kissing her. I leaned my forehead on hers. "Do you still want to do this?"

"Of course, I just want to make sure you do, too. After everything…"

I kissed her silent. It only took her a few seconds to relent this time, and she gave in with the force of a gale. Her fingers crawled around my back and unclasped my bra, freeing my breasts to the cool air of the room. My fingers trembled as I lifted her shirt over her head as well. Trembling out of fear or whatever this feeling was in my chest, I didn't know. All I knew was I needed to be inside of her. It was managing to crowd out every competing and baser need in my system.

Baser, yes. As I kissed her, and the warmth of our bodies pressed together, I recognized this as an ascension, as the thing that would bring me to a higher realm. The only thing, maybe.

With one arm behind her back, I flipped us both so she was on top. She pinned my shoulders to the bed and kissed me until I saw the very same fireworks I'd seen weeks ago at the skate park. I reached down and slipped her underwear off. She did the same with mine.

Then she, my radical skating pink warrior woman, made me forget. She made me forget with her fingers, with her mouth, pulling the need out of me like it was poison from a snakebite. She made me forget with her willing body, her attention, her love. She gave every ounce of herself to me, and like the greedy person I was, I took it.

When we were done, we lay next to one another. Casey's head rested on my chest, and I stroked her hair. My eyes were wide open, dry. It had been enough, in the moment. She had made me forget, but as she drifted off to sleep, the tugging of need returned, and I braced myself for a night of misery.

Chapter 21

SAVANNAH

I can't do this. I can't do this. Ican'tdothisIcan'tdothisIcan'tdothis.

"You can do this." Casey's eyes met mine in the mirror. It had only been a couple days since the story broke and it was gaining speed, twisting and turning like a rollercoaster ride. Now I was backstage at *The Sally Sullivan Show*, the lights of the makeup mirror illuminating every flaw in my face, out of my mind with nerves, and Casey was the one consoling me.

"This is a witch hunt," I said gripping the arms of the chair. "A distraction. It's not even helping our cause."

"Yes, it is," Casey said, her eyes open wide. She had left her hair down, parted it on the side, but it was hard to take her seriously with her pink hair and her belly shirt. Like a My Little Pony telling you it will be all right.

"It can't be. I'm supposed to be leading this and I'm unfocused."

"Given what happened I don't blame—"

"Digging up people from my childhood? My teen years? Really?"

"Can we have a minute?" Casey said, tapping the makeup woman on the shoulder. She nodded and left us alone. Casey knelt by my side and took my hand. I looked at the both of us in the mirror and saw I was bouncing my knee. *Fidgeting*. Oh, God. I needed… something. Something. But I didn't have anything because I had thrown it away and stupidly left the baggie at home.

"Why don't we stand up, like we did with that girl, Sam. Come on," Casey said, pulling me to my feet.

Maybe that woman from whom I had bought the blow was here. As I reluctantly stood, I glanced around, looking for her, but I didn't even remember her hair color. Maybe my makeup woman would know. Maybe it *was* the makeup woman.

"Put your hands up in the air."

"C'mon, Casey, that's dumb."

"It helped Sam," she said, grabbing my wrists, putting them up in the air. "It might help you, too."

Would my dealer recognize me if I looked at her? Would she hold my gaze a second longer than everyone else? My arms felt like rubbery noodles. Gently as I could, I tugged them away from Casey and took a step back. "That's not going to help me. Please, stop, Casey."

Casey swallowed and nodded.

I groaned inwardly. The last thing I needed was for her to pout. I buried my need for a boost and held out my hand to her. She put hers in mine and I brought her fingers to my lips. As her body came closer, mine turned on. I slid my hands down the side of her shorts.

"Here? Really?" she said against my fingers.

"No one's looking," I said, and replaced my fingers with my lips.

"I don't mind being a distraction for you," she

said into my lips, "But your makeup woman is going to be back any minute and you can't—"

"You're right. I can't be distracted." I shook my head, trying to make it all go away, and slid back into the chair, careful not to look at my reflection. What was I going to do? Now that the urge had entered my body, I knew I wasn't going to be able to make it go away by wishing it away. There wasn't time to orgasm it away, either. I ran my hands over my face.

I can't do this.

"Do you know what the most helpful thing you ever said to me was?"

"What?" I said through my hands.

"Pretend you're someone else. It works. It helps you get out of your own way. And I think it would help you, too, tonight. Your past didn't happen to you."

My past didn't happen to me. And neither was the present. This wasn't happening to me. I didn't feel this. My brain was tricking me into thinking I needed something I didn't. That was *it*. I pulled my hands away and gazed at my reflection objectively. The woman that looked back at me was serious. Beautiful, if a little tired looking.

"You are the most capable, strongest woman I've ever met." Casey spoke to the woman in the mirror. "You've got this. You know what to do. Trust yourself."

That was the key, wasn't it? Trusting myself?

So, what happens if your*self*, if the only thing you could find deep in your gut was an urge you couldn't control? Could you trust that when there was nothing else?

I couldn't help but think trusting it would lead to my destruction.

Chapter 21a

CASEY

People who say sex complicates things are wrong.

Sex was simple, even simpler than I imagined it would be with Sav. We'd never had a problem with attraction and it shot through our interactions in bed.

Whenever she had a hard day, like after her interview with Sally, I could give her that, at least. I could kiss away the tension from her shoulders, from her neck, from her jaw. It melted under my mouth.

Between the two of us, we were blanketing the town. My slot on *The Sally Sullivan Show* had put my cause on the map and brought more media attention and more requests for interviews everywhere I went. Once I'd done one, the rest got easier. People tended to ask the same questions, and when they didn't, I was relaxed enough to think of an answer. I was Pink, after all.

While the media blitz was energizing me, showering me with more attention than I'd ever had in my entire life and had always yearned for, it was drowning Sav. Every day I watched as a bit more of her slipped away, the cameras capturing a percentage of her soul each time. Every night I would try to give her a little of mine as I had some to spare at the time. She was the one I wanted to share it with.

However, my departure was impending. I had spent weeks circling around D.C., around Sav, like she was the sun and I had fallen into her gravitational orbit, but I was running out of space. After this, there was nowhere to go but north. I would be a few hours by car or train, then a few hours by plane, and then what? When I finished, would we be able to return to one another and start new? Would Sav survive alone until then? Did I want to leave her at all?

We'd become so tied together, so enmeshed, I was barely sure where I started and she ended. I didn't want to leave her, ever, and I wasn't sure how I had gotten there, but I was there now. And it was scary, but I loved it. I loved having someone count on me. I loved loving Sav.

I glanced over at her now, watching herself on the television in our hotel room. On the screen, she had a poise and a radiance. How she was able to do that, I wasn't sure, as she sat in front of me with almost none of that radiance left. A senator came on the screen, a smug cowboy-hat wearing senator, and told the pundit how she'd threatened him. How he'd thought she was on something she was so crazy.

"Why don't you turn that off?" I stood from the bed, walked over to her, and dug my fingers into the muscles of her shoulders.

Sav picked up my left hand and placed a kiss on the palm. Even this little movement was a gift. A gift she was giving from an almost empty chalice. "I'll be done in a few minutes. I've got to finish this to see where I could do better."

This comment marked a difference between me

and Sav. She prepared for every performance, milking it out of herself. Once I prepared for one, I relaxed for the rest. I wished she could do the same, though I knew it was pointless to tell her to relax. "You've done the best you can."

"They're right about me, you know. They're right about my family. How unstable we all are. How I was using people. I… I…"

I pushed my hands over her shoulders and rested my cheek against hers. "Have you seen the way people are talking about you? Real people on social media, not pundits on TV."

Sav shrugged, her body tense under my hands, like a stone statue. "You can't trust anything you see these days."

I pulled away. "Do you really believe that?"

"I don't know."

"If that's true, why are you believing these people?"

The screen flashed to a grainy video of a woman in a blood-orange dress dancing on the table. Anger surged within. "She didn't."

"What?" Sav turned back to the screen. "What the…?"

I reached over and slammed the laptop closed. "I'm going to track down the woman who filmed that and kill her myself."

"I don't remember… did I…?" She shook her head, her eyes glassy and empty.

"Yeah, but it wasn't that bad. I stopped you before you took off your dress."

One hand went to her mouth and one to her stomach. "What a mess I've made."

"It's fine. It's not a big deal."

"Can't you see? It's all true. All of it. True."

"No, it'll pass. You just need to give it time."

Sav squeezed her eyes shut, shaking her head. "Why don't you go to bed?"

I didn't want to leave her like this though I was tired. "Come with me."

"Soon."

My heart picked up. I told it to quiet down. It was just one night, and we were so close to freedom. So close to the vote. Who knew, maybe at that point Sav would come with me on my journey instead of me being a passenger on hers. "Are you sure you're all right?"

"Yeah," she said breathlessly.

I ambled back to the bed. The moment my head hit the pillow I fell asleep. It wasn't a restful sleep, not exactly. Occasionally, I would wake up and see the blue light of the laptop computer glowing off Sav's face, making her look like an alien come to Earth. In my dreams, she was an alien, a stranger in my life, forcing me into the light. In my dreams we were free from all the interviews and the attention, and we frolicked together.

I woke up sometime in the dead dark of early morning and found my little alien's chair empty. I could hear some noise coming from the bathroom. The latest iteration of my dream had featured Sav doing a spectacular back bend with me burying my face between her legs. It had been so realistic I was now slick as a slip and slide.

Smiling, I decided to use the element of surprise in my favor. I tiptoed to the bathroom, my chest fluttering, my center pulling me toward her like we were connected by some invisible thread. At the door, I hesitated for just a moment before my glee pushed me inside. I wrenched open the door.

A slow-motion progression followed. A flash of images. Sav bent over the sink, her shoulders hunched up to her ears. Sav swinging around, a credit card in her left hand. A smudge of white dust beneath her nose. A flash of fear, then anger in her features.

Then Sav was gone, and in her place was my mother. She was burning, the house was burning, and I couldn't get her to wake up. *Wake up, wake up wake up.*

This couldn't be happening again. This was just a dream. It had to be a dream. This wasn't my Sav, the woman who'd taken hold of my heart and chased after me again and again, never letting me run. I backed out of the bathroom, slamming the door behind me. In the process, I shut it on my toe and let out a yelp.

I wasn't dreaming. This only made me hold on to the knob harder, shutting the woman I had seen inside. I looked around the room, at the chair where Sav had been sitting. I hadn't imagined it. That was Sav in there. But how could it be? She was a successful businesswoman, not a common drug addict.

"Casey? Open the door, please. Let me explain."

Sav's voice was small, but definitely hers. It only made all of this more real. I squeezed the handle of the door and shook my head.

What am I supposed to do? What the hell do I

do?

My center was still slick with want, but my head was no longer in it.

"Casey," Sav said, a little tremor in her voice. "I didn't mean for you to see me like that. I'm just doing it to get by for a night, it's not like I'm addicted or anything."

It's not like I'm addicted or anything. Those words had been stronger, tinged with disgust. I'd heard them a thousand times from the mouth of my mother. Usually followed by, I can quit anytime I want. Usually followed by not quitting, near overdoses, and destruction. Those words brought me back to myself. Back to the moment. My grip loosened on the handle, and I backed away.

I had been on *her* journey, but I wasn't willing to go crashing into the trees with her.

Crash. Too late. Everything in my stomach soured, heaving upward like a bucket drawn from the bottom of the well. I paced one way, then the other, never finding the pocket of air I sought. Crushed lungs. I couldn't breathe. I couldn't think. I couldn't…

I walked away from the door. Sav's phone sat on the desk. I unlocked it based on a combination I'd seen her do a thousand times and found Lori's number. My hands shook so hard I almost dropped the phone.

No.

I dialed Lori. The call went to voicemail.

"Hi, Lori," I said in a hushed voice. "You don't know me, but Savannah's in trouble. I think she's doing drugs. I'm not sure what to do about that." My voice cracked on the last words. I became a little girl again, calling 911 at the side of my mother. Damn her. Damn Savannah. Damn it all. "She's at the Grand Hyatt. Somebody needs to do something." I threw the phone down on the desk.

Savannah stormed out as I was gathering my things to go.

"Are you leaving? Just because of a little…"

"I spent the first years of my life taking care of an addict when she should've been taking care of me, and I spent the next decade dealing with the consequences. Why the hell do you think I would spend one more minute with an addict?"

"I'm not an addict."

It was all coming into focus now. The party. How tired she looked and how she never seemed to sleep. And the last crowning image, the snorting of cocaine. It was all coming together to create a new image, a nasty image. I didn't think I could ever look at her again, never mind have a relationship with her.

I turned away and dragged toward the door, my bag slung over my shoulders, my skates hitting against my back

"Please don't go. Please."

Savannah's voice was so desperate, so broken, part of me wanted to stay. I might have, even a year ago, but Savannah had made me stronger. She made me see my past didn't have to define me. She made me see I didn't have to relive it, which was why I was leaving.

It took more courage than I'd ever possessed to walk out the door, but I did. I knew doing so would define my life. It was a turning point. It was the first thing I had done not out of fear, but out of courage. Sure, I was running away from something, but I was running toward something, too. Me.

Chapter 22

SAVANNAH

Casey's leaving wasn't the end. It was only a step in the long walk where she would run away, and I would chase after her and drag her back to me. This was an easy fix. It was simply a case of explaining to her all the facts she didn't have. How what she'd witnessed had been the first time. How it was temporary, only a boost so I can get through this week and the vote. How I would never do it again because of my brother. Because I knew where addiction led. Because, like her, I'd seen it all before. I'd seen how it could take over someone's life, destroy it and the lives of those closest to them.

Once I explained it to her, she would understand. She would come back and we would kiss and make up and I would finish this vote and win and we would skate off together into the sunset. The only problem was, Casey wasn't answering her phone. And I even had her phone number now, as opposed to the beginning of our relationship, but it seemed it was off. As the morning progressed, the number became entirely unreachable. Disconnected.

Disconnected.

That shook me, to be honest, but it was just another hurdle I had to clear. I could track her down somehow, through friends or some other means. I had my ways.

Since the opioid story I'd crafted had become my family's drug story, I'd barely stepped foot in the office. I'd spent most my time in my hotel room and on news sets. As I made my way through the halls that Monday morning, I noticed how dull it was. It could really use a redesign. Maybe after this vote was through, I'd put some color on the walls. Some art more interesting than Monet prints, perhaps.

Or maybe I would find some real freedom. Maybe I would take a long vacation if Tim would let me. If Casey had taught me anything it was that this didn't have to be my story. This didn't have to be how I lived my life. I had a choice. Ultimately, it was all up to me.

Despite what had happened earlier in the morning, I hadn't been in such a good mood for weeks. After Casey had left, I worked in a focused frenzy. I even felt a smile cross my face as I edged into my office, ready to take whatever came at me. Except for what I actually found there.

Lori leaned on my desk, her arms folded, her face a painting of her feelings. Fear mixed with determination. But I didn't have long to dwell on that before I heard a familiar voice call my name.

"Savannah."

My head swiveled to the couple to my right. I didn't know if it was the cocaine, or just that I was plain old done being sad and depressed anymore. It wasn't that I didn't understand what was happening. I understood perfectly. This could only mean one thing.

I turned toward Lori. "You bitch."

My eyes practically flashed red as I turned on my

heels and clicked out of the office, my steps echoing on the walls.

Lori was close behind. She caught my arm with a surprisingly strong grip. But I was stronger, strengthened by rage, and ripped my arm away. I wasn't so lucky with my father, who wrapped me up in a bear hug and dragged me back.

I wouldn't let it go this easily. I kicked and screamed and fought my father, but nothing I did helped. His arms tightened around my torso as he dragged me backward into the conference room. My conference room. The room where I had closed so many deals. I caught a flash of Tim as he closed the door behind us. He was in on this, too? Traitors and betrayers. That's what they all were.

My father dropped me in the corner of the room. It felt like I was in a boxing ring. I squared off, facing my opponent. Faking a calm I didn't feel, I walked back to the door and tried the knob. It was locked.

"Let me out of here," I said.

"No one can hear you, Savannah," my father said. My mother stared at a wall, stoic. Figured.

I pounded on the door, kicking it, but nothing was helping.

"You can kick and scream all you want, but we're not letting you out of here unless you agree to go to rehab," Lori said.

"Rehab?" What the fuck was she doing here, anyway? It was none of her business. I turned my gaze on her, like I could shoot darts from my eyes. "Oh, I see. Little Miss Lori is growing a spine."

Lori lifted her chin, a pathetic answer to my snide comment. Behind her, a tear ran down my mother's cheek. What was she crying for? I kicked the door one more time. "I'm not going to rehab."

Even then, at the height of my rage, I recognized kicking and punching the door probably wouldn't get me anywhere. I needed to change tactics. I needed to treat this as any other challenge I was faced with. I needed to slip into my role as The Closer to get my way.

Gathering all my energy, I pulled out the chair at the conference table and sat down. My father bristled like an angry porcupine, pacing the room, his face tomato red. Mom wiped away her single tear. Her graying blond hair was swooped up into a French twist. Her eyes looked perfect, if a little red-rimmed, her waterproof makeup holding strong. This was better. This was the mother I remembered.

I didn't even look at Lori. She didn't matter here. She wasn't in my life anymore and didn't deserve the attention. I was reasonably sure it was her who called my parents like a tattletale in second grade. She took a seat next to me.

My father closed his fingers over the top of the chair opposite her, the pockets under his eyes deep. "I can't believe you would do this, after everything with your brother. I can't believe you would put your mother through this again."

"Since when do you and Mom give a shit about me?" He didn't know anything about my life, and I needed to set them all straight. "You've got it all wrong."

They all looked at me with rapt attention. "I was having trouble staying focused. I went to a doctor and he prescribed me Adderall. I only take it when I need an extra boost. I don't have a problem."

"So you need an extra boost every day?" Lori asked.

The back of my neck burned. I flattened my hands to the table, so they wouldn't start tapping out my excess energy or land straight on Lori's face in fist form.

"Plus, I know you've been doing cocaine."

I rolled my eyes. "You don't do cocaine. Let's be specific. You snort cocaine and…"

Cocaine. She hadn't seen me do cocaine. The only person that had seen me do that was… Oh God. "I can't believe she called you."

"I can't believe you did that to her. How could you?"

I straightened, tired of being accused of doing everything to everybody. "You don't know anything about us."

"I've seen you both all over the news. I know your handiwork and I can put two and two together. She lost her mother because of drugs. She lost her house because of drugs. She lost everything, and now you're flaunting it in her face. But I should've known. No one's ever accused you of being nice, Savannah."

It wasn't a decision, but a reaction. I flew out of my chair, my hands outstretched, and they just tightened around her neck. Then I was on top of her, on the floor, and my mother was sobbing, shrieking, and my father was pulling me away, and I was lashing out like a tigress whose cubs have been attacked. Someone banged on the door, a muffled voice shouting through. I felt like my arms were made of steel, but when I saw Lori's terrified face, stricken, the vein popping out of the side of her forehead, I backed away on my own.

"We clearly can't talk about this right now," my father said. "I know what it looks like when someone's strung out, and you're not my Savannah right now. You're going to sit here and come down until you're ready to talk."

I sneered. "You're giving me a timeout?"

"You never really knew when you needed one before. So, yes, I'm giving you a timeout. We'll be right outside in case you need us."

They filed out one by one. They brought me food and water and then locked me inside like I was some kind of prisoner. My mind raged, and sometimes the rage spilled out in a groan or a fist on the table. As hours passed, however, I began to calm. Lori's words started to pierce me, a tiny prick at first, but one that grew into a scrape, then a festering sore.

It was all bad, but the part about Casey was worst.

What had I done? I had made Casey trust me, I practically forced her to trust me. And then I had demolished that trust like it was a worthless wall of shit. My hands began to shake, and exhaustion overwhelmed me.

The yearning deep inside for just a hit took me over, and for the first time I saw it clearly. I had a problem. And before I could fix anything, before I could close any further deals, including the most important deal of my life—pleading for Casey's forgiveness—I had to do something about it.

Chapter 23

CASEY

I thought leaving before it got worse would make me feel like a hero who had conquered a dragon and returned home. So I hadn't been sucked in again. I hadn't tried to make someone love me who would always love something or someone else more. I didn't let myself become second best to a drug. That meant I won, right?

Apparently, not so much. My days were filled with activity. I'd moved on to New Jersey, New York, Connecticut. In many of those places, the local news shows wanted me, just like Sav said. My dreams were becoming real.

Like before, I made new friends. I attended parties, book readings, concerts… I never said no when someone extended an invitation. But while my body kept moving, my heart stood still.

I only felt the pain of the thousand tiny cuts to my heart when I stopped. The image of Sav bent over the sink wasn't even the worst of it. Worse was the lying. The deception. I saw now what I couldn't see before. It went all the way back to the beginning. To the party, and the bushes, and the dancing on the table.

Could I trust anything she had ever said?

Could I trust she loved me?

Had I been just a toy to her? A project she could

mold into her image and toss out when she was done?

How could she have done that to me? She knew my background. My story. She knew and she still chased after me, kept me close. All those news stories about her had been *true*.

Why hadn't I sensed it earlier? I knew the signs like they were engraved in my DNA. An inability to remain still. A single-minded focus. Mood swings. *Check. Check. Check.*

Had I actually been attracted to it on some level? Trying to get my mother's love again or some bullshit like that?

One morning, I woke up in a dripping sweat and remembered it wasn't the real Savannah that had just been rolling around with me in bed. It was the one of my dreams. The sob rose my chest, and a cry from my throat.

I couldn't do this anymore. Not alone. My brain was just going around in circles. I dialed Clari, my chest still heaving, out of breath.

When she didn't pick up, I called her again. And again. And again. The fourth time, a groggy voice answered.

"Hello?"

Only then did I realize Clari was on the west coast, in Portland. It was four AM her time. "I'm sorry, I'll call you back later."

"Casey? Is everything okay?"

"Yes." I didn't want to worry her too much, but my voice wavered on the word "No. No, everything's not all right. I'm so sorry. I shouldn't have called you. I—"

"Slow down, sweetheart." Clari's voice was soothing, soft, and I didn't miss the hint of worry in it. I had never cried to her, not in all our years as friends. Not with all the things that had happened to me. I had never, ever cried. "Why did you tell me to go for it with Savannah? Why?"

"What happened?" I recognized my words were too angry. I was vacillating wildly between anger and depression these days, in these in between moments. Clari didn't deserve either. I sniffed, wiping the tears away from my eyes, though they only produced more to replace them so it was a fruitless effort.

"I caught her snorting… something… I think it was coke in the bathroom."

"Oh, my God. That's horrible. I'm sorry."

"We're not together anymore. Obviously. I don't know how to get past it."

Clari didn't reply. Her silence troubled me. I could hear her breathing, but she wasn't saying anything.

"Did you hear me?"

"Yeah, I'm just trying to… Why do you think she was doing that?"

"Does it matter?"

"I don't know. I tend to think if someone's struggling with addiction, it means they're struggling with deeper issues. I know it's a deal-breaker. I'm not saying you should have stayed."

"Then what are you saying?"

"I'm just saying there might be something going on in her life that makes her want to escape. Do you know what it is?"

Was it me? No, it wasn't me. I was sure of that. It

was her brother's overdose coming out in the media. It was her long work hours. The interviews. The stress had weighed on her. Had I only added to the stress? Terror gripped my stomach. What if she had collapsed in the hotel room, overdosed on something or other? I had left when she needed me most. "Oh, my God."

"Don't do that," Clari said. "This is not about you. It's not your fault."

There was no substitute for the real Clari. I called her thinking she would say something like *to hell with her, you deserve better*. The Clari in my head would never have said what the real Clari did because that voice was me, someone without the years of psychological training.

"I'm not saying you should go back to her. Or that you did the wrong thing in leaving. It might've been exactly the right choice. Everyone's different. You know..." She hesitated.

I tried to pull myself back from the edge of the cliff to listen to her. "What?"

"I had a little problem with alcohol last year. I ended up in the hospital and everything. Paul helped me through it. I don't know what I would've done without him."

"Why didn't you tell me?"

"We weren't speaking often at the time. Remember? What I want to convey is I really appreciate the chance he gave me."

Wasn't the definition of love getting sucked in? I wasn't sure how I could do it without losing myself in the drama of the situation. "I don't think I could do that."

"I'm here for you whatever you decide. In fact, need a place to crash far away from D.C.?"

"No, I'm good. Thanks." She was so sweet. I was lucky to have her. I took in a long breath and let it out. "What was wrong in your life?"

"Hm?"

"You said if someone was addicted something was wrong. What was wrong in yours?"

Clari let out a sigh of her own. "I hated my job. It's so pedestrian, really, but it made me miserable every day. I constantly wanted to escape. Alcohol seemed easiest."

I fiddled with the blanket in my lap. "I wish you were here to give me a hug. I wish I was there to give you a hug."

"Me too, sweetheart. Me too." A pause settled over the line. Cari yawned and cleared her throat. "Hey, do you mind if I go back to bed now, since you called me at an ungodly hour?"

I laughed. It was small, an echo of my real laugh, but it was the first time I'd even come close. "Of course, I'm sorry again. Say hi to Paul for me."

We exchanged our goodbyes and hung up the phone.

I flopped back on the bed.

Clari had a point, one I wasn't sure she meant to make. I had been thinking this was all about me, but it wasn't. It was about Sav. It was her problem, her life that was weighed down. That only made it worse. It meant I couldn't do anything fix it. It meant I was still in bed, alone, in love with a woman who may not ever be able to love me in return. Would I ever get over Savannah and love again?

Chapter 24

SAVANNAH

The sun made a dappled puzzle on the dirt path under my feet, a breeze gently shushing through the canopy of trees. The air was heavy with the scent of the roses spread out in a riot of colors all around me.

"How are you?" the woman beside me asked.

I'd been doing a lot of thinking and feeling lately. "I'm okay," I said, dragging my canvas shoe along the path, kicking a rock.

"Are you nervous about leaving?"

"Not really." I hesitated before taking my next step, as if physically stopping myself from the lie. Truth was a big thing for me now. The only thing keeping me sane. "A little."

"What part scares you? Going back to work?"

"Not really. I can handle that."

"Then what?"

"Who wants to go back to an office to fix other people's problems when you can sit in a rose garden all day and talk about yourself?" I joked.

Dr. Ashley laughed. She was young, perhaps younger than me even, but that didn't make me respect her any less. She was practical, open, and a good listener—all the things I needed to help myself heal.

I took a seat at the next bench, facing fat thorned bushes with peach flowers. The roses were at the height of bloom. In a way, they had mirrored my stay here. Closed and tightly wrapped when I arrived, now opening to the sun. Dr. Ashley took the seat next to me.

"I've spoken to you about Casey," I said, after a long pause.

"The woman you were seeing, yes."

"How do I… how do I go about apologizing to her? How can I get her back?"

Dr. Ashley sat with her hands folded, exuding calm. Meanwhile, my heart was hammering at the mention of Casey. I'd had weeks of rehab to think about her, to soak in all the good things she brought to my life. She'd given me a taste of pure joy, of a real life. And what had I done? I'd crashed hard enough for us both.

"You can only control your end of things, Savannah."

"I know, but I've worked so hard here. I'm clean. I think I can stay clean. How do I make her understand that?"

"You don't. You betrayed her trust. She needs time."

"How much?"

"I don't know. As much as it takes. The only thing you can do is apologize and wait."

Waiting. If that didn't drive me to use *something* I don't know what would. I was obviously not cured, not yet. Though my body was no longer addicted, my mind still searched for the calm and focus. Is this how Carson, my brother, felt going in and out of rehab? The itch. The need for some semblance of sanity. For the first time, I understood.

"Should I track her down and apologize in person?"

"Do you think that's a good idea?"

Yes. It's what I wanted. The old Savannah would have made everything okay. She would find what she needed—Casey's forgiveness—and brick-by-brick she would pull down any walls Casey had erected. It was a thick wall. I'd tried to contact Casey multiple times, I'd even found her friends and tried to track her down through them, but I'd heard nothing back. She wanted nothing to do with me.

"She doesn't want to see me," I admitted.

"Then maybe you should write a letter."

A letter. My heart lifted, skipped a beat. A letter. Maybe that was my way to get to her. But how would I find her?

That session stuck with me. I left rehab later that week, but not before I walked into the common room and found a familiar face on the news.

Her hair was purple now, a little longer, long enough to tuck behind her ears, but she was still as stunning as ever. Still quirky. Still weird.

The noise deadened around me like someone had turned off the volume of the voices in the room. All I could hear was her voice as she answered the same questions she always got. She looked both strange and familiar, both mine and not mine.

No, not mine at all, I reminded myself. I had destroyed the relationship. Horror surfaced in my stomach, threatening to come out my throat.

I eased down into a chair. I needed to do something with my hands. *Something*.

If you were looking at me from the outside, you

may not have noticed I was tuned to every word on the TV. You might've thought I belonged to a mental institution, rather than rehab, the way I was frantically putting together pieces of construction paper in front of me. It must've only lasted a few minutes, these local news interviews always did, but by the end of the interview I had made what I'd wanted.

As a final question, the reporter asked her about a book deal she'd gotten with Simon & Schuster.

I put down my preschool-aged tools and stared at the screen, beaming despite myself. She had gotten a book deal. Good for her. The last time I was this proud was when she had done her first interview. But she had done this all by herself. I hadn't had a hand in it, and for that I was even prouder.

Making amends, it was part of this process. I'd done it with Lori, with my parents, but I hadn't done it with the person I loved most. In part, because I hadn't known how to reach her. Now I did. The book deal meant she had a publisher. Which meant I could send something to her, care of them. It wasn't perfect, but I wasn't striving for perfection any longer.

I was striving for good enough.

Now I knew where to send my letter. Hopefully it *would* be good enough.

...

CASEY

Some days all I could do was think about Savannah. Other days, I barely thought of her at all. I took this as a sign of progress. Over a month after our break-up, I was having a particularly good Savannah day, or non-Savannah day, as the case may have been in actuality, when I went to meet with my editor about the first chapter of my memoir.

Though my editor had assured me this was common, I was nervous. The entire way into New York City from Rhode Island, where I had just been skating, I practically tapped a hole in the top of my knee, my finger a little jackhammer of nerves. Savannah had entered my mind then, a vision in a perfectly pressed black suit on the other side of the glass coffee table. *Pretend you're Pink*. The trick still worked. It was Pink who walked into the building that day, not Casey.

The meeting went well enough. The chapter was rough, but my editor gave me helpful notes and by the end of the meeting I was pretty sure I could give her a stronger second draft. The publishing company was behind me, supporting me. I felt it more than ever after my meeting with the editor.

As I was on my way out with my long list of notes in hand, she stopped me. "Oh, Casey, hold on. I have a letter here for you. Your first fan mail."

"Fan mail?" That was something I would have to get used to. The fact people actually sought me out, even now after months of being on TV and a steady stream of interviews, after being offered a book deal, made me feel like an impostor. Like I didn't deserve it. I'd learned to stop doubting it out loud—people didn't seem to appreciate it—but my body betrayed me, my neck growing hot with embarrassment.

I waited until I was out of her office to examine

the envelope. It had a return address from Virginia, but no name. It had been posted a week ago. It was in a large, thin manila envelope.

Curiosity got the best me, and I closed myself in the bathroom with my fan letter. I ripped the envelope open and out slipped a construction paper house with a heart pasted in the middle. My own heart melted at the construction, thinking it was from a foster kid who had received a bag of items from Voices for Love, or had seen me on TV or something, but when I flipped it over, the writing was small and neat. It was that of an adult, or at least an older kid. My excitement turned to ash in my mouth as I began to read.

Casey,

You're wonderful. And now I know I love you. My heart is yours. What you do with it is up to you. All I have to say is I'm sorry.

No signature. This could only be from one person. Savannah. I took out my phone and searched the return address. A rehab facility popped up. She had written to me from rehab. She hadn't begged. Or explained. She had simply apologized. My hand loosened from where it was clutching the edge of the paper. I smoothed out the wrinkles in the roof of the paper house.

I'd finally got somewhere on my own and she was writing me a message. A message of love. Why would she do that? If she really cared about me wouldn't she just leave me alone? If she'd had known how well I was doing without her, which she did as she had sent the letter to my publisher, why did she insist on dragging me down?

I'd been running my hands over the house. Over the heart. And my own gave one strong beat. Savannah.

Chapter 25

SAVANNAH

I'm not going to lie—I hoped for a reply from Casey. A letter, or a phone call, or a blimp or a message in my dreams. I hoped for something, and every day I got nothing. The thing about hope, though, was that it just wouldn't quit. No matter how many days passed, it gnawed into my gut.

And I let it.

I was letting lots of things gnaw into my gut these days. I hadn't felt so much, maybe ever. Even before the drugs, I'd dulled the pain and filled the empty spaces with work. Even in school with my friends. Now, I made a point to leave long empty swaths of time when I had nothing planned.

It was part of the Improve Savannah Method.

It wasn't so hard when I was in rehab. There was time to spare. But when I got out and inserted myself back into D.C. life, the pull was almost immediate. My job was like a cyclone sucking everything else up into it. While the opioid bill had passed without me —despite me—there were others. There would always be others. Always another wrong to fix, another inefficiency to close, another life to save. Everything was of *the utmost importance* every time. Every day. It was exhausting.

Though I had been tempted to quit outright early on, I realized that was just another knee-jerk response. I needed a stable and familiar routine. Finding new work would add stress. Plus, I was doing a good thing, working hard for good people. I just couldn't let it destroy me this time around. So I pulled back. Way back. Tim didn't offer me the promotion. He apologized profusely when he told me, but I didn't want it now, anyway. It was time to watch. To watch, learn, and listen until I found what to do next.

Sixty days, eighty days, one hundred days sober and watching. Listening to my gut. Dealing with the temptations and stresses of daily life one moment at a time. Sometimes, usually unbidden, a great sadness bloomed in my chest. I knew it was about Casey. Rather than berating myself as I once might have done, I consoled my inner self as she sobbed and yearned. We mourned together and healed one another like that. Watching. Waiting for a sign. I wrote Casey letters during this time, telling her how I felt. Sending them to her publishing company. Not knowing whether she had received them.

As the days progressed, all my watching produced a thought. In my job, I only saw the end of the process. The hurried, pressure-ridden part. I was The Closer, but I always had to work with what was given to me, no matter how flawed.

I wanted to create something. To take something from a seed of an idea and bring it through to the end.

Tim loved the idea when I pitched it to him, and I followed it up with another suggestion. "Let's start with the foster care system."

Tim raised an eyebrow, but I explained, and

convinced him it was a good idea. He even admitted it himself, but as he did so, he glanced at me from the side of his eyes, as if looking at me straight-on would put me on attack. I didn't blame him—he had seen me on the worst day of my life. I was surprised I still had a job after all that.

"Go ahead. Ask," I said.

"Are you sure you're ready?"

I shrugged. "I don't know."

"I agree it's a great thing to focus on, but I can give this to someone else to spearhead. I don't want you to risk—"

I placed a hand on his sinewy forearm. "This is my project. I need to see it through. I'll be fine, and if I'm starting to feel too stressed, I'll tell you right away. I'll step back. I promise."

Tim nodded a little too much. "Okay. Let's set some targets and meeting dates to check in every so often."

I agreed to the oversight. It would be good to have someone there to work with.

The letters hadn't been enough. They'd been everything I could give, but now I felt ready to give more. This was my gift to Casey. The manifestation of my love. If she didn't take this as an apology, I didn't know what else I would do.

...

CASEY

I couldn't remember the last time I had remained in one place for so long. I had finished my tour of the country—all fifty-two states in a year plus D.C.—and had decided to settle in a town in New

Jersey just outside the city. I couldn't live *in* New York City. It was a nice enough place to visit, but there were too many people and not enough room to skate, so I settled in the 'burbs.

It was *so* not me. And *so* temporary. But I still wasn't sure what *was* me. Maybe I was meant to be a nomad, wandering the Earth, spreading joy.

There was plenty to do around, plenty of places to see. I could drive up north and hike in the Catskills, or I could do anything I wanted in the city, but I found myself savoring the stillness of writing. It was just me and my past, most of the time, but it wasn't torturous this time around. The act of writing it down was cathartic. I could almost see myself dragging the memories from my brain and setting them down on the paper as if they were concrete things. Once they took up residence on the paper they no longer weighed on me.

When I wasn't writing, I did *normal* things like watch TV, attend protests, and keep tabs on Voices for Love. Voices for Love was actually based in the city, and at the end of my skate they threw me a party. I'd become friends with some of the people in the upper ranks, or friendly, I should say. No one had come close to replacing Clari, yet. I wasn't sure it was possible, but it was nice to have some people I could go out with.

One night, I was having drinks in a bar in Manhattan with one of the women—Helena—when she grabbed my arm. "You will never believe what happened today."

Helena wasn't given to drama, or over-excited exclamations, so I was surprised by her tone.

"What?" I asked.

She let go of my arm. I had been so infrequently touched lately that a sense of coolness rushed in to fill the empty space. *I miss Sav so much,* my brain said, before I shut down the thought.

"I got a phone call today from a lobbyist who's trying to pass a bill to protect foster kids. She wants to do a multi-pronged approach that would focus on connections and supporting the kids in their grief, and public education on the issues."

My heart dropped. It could have been a million people who had put forward that bill. It didn't have to be Savannah. It probably wasn't. She had written me dozens of letters in the past few months talking about her life, and she had never mentioned anything like this. Wouldn't she have told me?

"What was her name?" I asked, the question sticking in my throat.

"Something… Georgia?"

"Savannah?"

"Yes! That's it. Savannah Burns. Do you know her?"

I swallowed and swallowed, trying to calm my nerves, trying to stop the pink martini from coming back up. "A little," I said, hedging. "What did she want?"

Helena gave me a side-glance, but she didn't press me. Maybe she thought she didn't know me well enough for that, and I was glad. I didn't think I could talk about Savannah any more.

"She's trying to get buy-in from the major related organizations. It's the most comprehensive bill I've ever seen, but also far too idealistic. Nothing will come of it, most likely."

"I wouldn't count Savannah out."

In the dim light of the bar, I could only see the whites of Helena's eyes get better. "What do you know?"

"Nothing," I said, glad for the dim light situation now as the heat crawled up my chest.

"You know more than you're letting on. Come on!"

"I—I just know Savannah is a bull dog. If she's behind a project, you can be damn sure it'll go somewhere. She won't give up until she has to."

As evidenced by the dozens of letters I kept in a shoe box in my apartment. Letter after letter, most of them postmarked from an address in D.C. All of them detailed how she missed me, and how she was sorry for what she had done. None of them begging for me to come back, but all of them saying on a deeper level, *I am stable. I can be your home.* Just like the first letter. This was the first time I had spoken her name in a long time, and it scraped through my throat like it was a knife.

Savannah. Savannah.

"She seems very familiar with the issues. Do you know if she was a foster kid herself or knows anyone? I didn't want to ask her on the first phone call."

"No," I said, absently. "Yes."

I dropped my head in my hands. Hiding myself from others had long since become boring, and I missed the intimacy. Any intimacy. I turned to Helena. "Me. She and I had a little… thing."

Helena slammed her palms on the table. "You

know a sympathetic lobbyist and didn't tell me?"

"It's complicated."

"How? Ugh. I'm sorry. Sometimes I'm too nosy for my own good."

Where to start? The only person who knew the story was Clari, and I'd lost track of how much I'd told her. Plus, she and Paul were planning a wedding, so she didn't exactly have a lot of time to talk. Oh, why not.

"We dated for a while, but it got… we didn't end well. She…"

Helena stared unblinking, her eyes wide as Goofy's. The bartender offered us another drink, but she waved him away. "Go on," she said, her full attention on me.

I couldn't tell her about the drugs. It might destroy Helena's view of her. Savannah had been through rehab and she deserved a fresh start, at least with her career. "She did something I couldn't forgive at the time."

Helena frowned and I didn't blame her. The way I'd stated it made it seem like I was the bad guy.

"Huh," she said.

"What?"

"Nothing."

"What?" I said, placing my hands on the bar. I was close to regretting I'd told her anything at all.

"If you're her only tie, then it seems like she's making quite the effort to apologize. What did she do? Was it really so bad?"

"It was bad enough." I'd been thinking about this, though. As the letters had come in they had worn me down bit by bit. At first, I had tried to block out all thoughts of her, but now I found her seeping into my brain. Not in a negative way, not in the hate-fest way she had entered them originally. After my discussion with Clari and her letters one line kept running through my head. *She didn't do this to you.*

Sav's drug use was her problem, not mine.

"I wish my boyfriend would apologize to me with a new law." Helena pouted, her hands around her drink.

I changed the subject to sports, which Helena loved, but I continued to think about Sav. No one had ever given anything to me, not really. And she hadn't called and rubbed it in my face. She hadn't desperately sought my approval on this. In a quiet way, she was moving forward with something she knew I cared about

She had been wearing me down for months, but in that moment, I felt my heart flip. God, I loved her. I still loved her. If I had known love would be this painful, I never would have skated into that bathroom.

Chapter 26

SAVANNAH

Two years passed. Two years of challenges and working hard and pain and joy and lots of boring moments and grinding moments. Two years of sobriety and mending relations and no Casey. She had to know about the law by now. We'd been working hard on it, finding financial backers, coming up with the proposed changes, lobbying congress to introduce it into committee, getting it accepted. Passing committee.

No one had yet opposed it, and how could they? Democrat, Republican, they all wanted to be seen as fighting for children. Some would argue on the technical aspects, on the funding, but we had plans for all of it. I was almost confident it would pass.

The week before the vote was to be held on the All Children Deserve A Family Act, we held a gala. It was a typical D.C. gala given by a wealthy donor— over-the-top glamorous, all the big names. I was slated to speak, to talk about how I had spearheaded the process, and I was more nervous than I had ever been at one of these things.

It wasn't the speaking. That came easily enough. It was the possibility of seeing Casey Day for the first time in years. We had invited her to read from her memoir. She had accepted. These were the facts. The rest left me in muddled confusion.

I gave myself a once-over in the mirror. A sapphire floor-length one-shoulder gown that shimmered in the light hugged my body. My hair fell in loose curls over my shoulders.

"You're going to kill it," I said to my reflection in the mirror. "You're going to be okay," I said more reasonably. Since the crash, as I'd come to call it, I'd learned to adjust my expectations. To trust my body when it said no. It was saying no now, but that was out of fear, and fear wasn't allowed to control me any longer.

Yet it certainly tried hard. I was scared out of my ever-living mind to see Casey. If the underarms of my dress were higher, they would have been soaked through already. I picked at my hair, separating the curls.

It was time to go.

My car arrived, and I slipped inside. The entire ride I repeated to myself *you're going to be okay. You'll be all right. It's okay.*

But was it? I'd written more than sixty letters to Casey and hadn't heard anything back. I'd been single the entire time and celibate as a nun. Tonight I would see her, and though it had been such a long time and I had no reason to think I had a chance, a tiny part of me pulsed. *Maybe.*

This was the biggest test I'd had yet. My heart resided in my throat the entire ride there.

I didn't have to wait long to see her.

My car pulled up to the gala venue ten minutes before seven, early so I would have time to prepare my speech and hopefully avoid the arriving rush. I thanked my driver, got out of my car, and scanned the pavilion. My eyes stuttered and stopped over a woman with chin-length blonde hair.

Our gazes held. The car left, and I stayed put at the edge of the road. Though she looked so different, I had known who she was immediately. My heart skipped a beat, my stomach dropped straight down to my ankles. The wind blew my curls over my eyes and I wiped them away, just so I could continue looking at her.

She wore a burgundy dress, short, with straps over the heart tattoo on her chest. I noticed now, her hair wasn't all blonde. She had a streak of burgundy running down the side of her head. A part of me, my soul, ran toward her and slung my arms around her neck, sinking my lips into hers.

My body, weighed down by fear and regret, stayed put. She would have to make the first move.

The pressure of waiting rendered my lungs useless. I could only drag in little gulps of air. Minutes may have passed like this, or maybe seconds. Time meant nothing to me.

Please, I begged in my mind. *Stay. Say something.*

She only stared. I dragged my gaze away, breaking contact so I wouldn't disintegrate to ashes under her burning gaze. It was enough for me to take a full breath. It only lasted a few seconds, maybe, but when I turned back, she was gone. Vanished. Like a ghost.

It took everything I had not to crumple to the sidewalk and cry my eyes out. It took more than I had to walk toward the venue and enter the place where the woman I wanted most but couldn't have resided. I'd thought it would come down to a moment. I just hadn't fully prepared myself for if the moment was devastating.

...

CASEY

She was more beautiful than ever. Softer, more relaxed somehow, though I could sense she was startled to see me. She had to know I would be there. It was her event, after all. To tell the truth, I was surprised to see her so soon. Surprised and also relieved. I'd thought, maybe, the night in the hotel had ruined her for me forever. I thought the image of her hunched over the sink, melding into the image of my mother, would be it for us. The end. Done.

But when I'd seen her outside, she was just… Savannah. Maybe it was because I'd had two years to process the incident. Maybe it was because of her letters. I didn't know. It was both welcome and terrifying at the same time. Terrifying because if I had forgiven her, what was stopping us from getting back together? From going down that path again?

Absofuckinglutely nothing.

If this law had been all a scam to get me back—it was working. It hadn't, at first. I kept thinking she would crack under the pressure of it. Now we were only a week away from finding out whether it would go through. It would. She'd done it. And it was the sexiest thing anyone had ever done for me.

When she'd broken eye contact, I couldn't trust myself any longer. If I had gone to her, we would have ended up in a back alley or a bathroom somewhere, and I didn't want that with her. We both deserved better than that. Just because our relationship started in the crapper didn't mean it had to end there. Or start there again? Gosh, this was so complicated.

As I walked into the museum where the fundraiser for the bill was being held, I questioned all my choices. I should have called her earlier, worked this out. Why had I pushed off our first meeting for such an important night?

Tonight also marked my first reading from my book. It wasn't out yet, not quite, but it was the perfect night to preview it. I was nervous as hell for that alone, and then I had to go and add to it by leaving our first meeting post everything to the same night as the reading?

Excess energy coursed through my limbs. If only I had my skates on instead of these horrid heels, then I could skate some of the energy out, or at least play around on my skates until I fell on my ass and flashed half the place and laughed.

Inside, the place looked like a starry-night-themed prom on steroids. Sparkle lights lined the tables. The women wore expensive gowns that sparkled in the soft light and hairstyles that cost more than my entire ensemble. I hadn't attended my prom for a reason, and now I remembered why.

I found my place at a table where I knew no one and took my seat, thumbing through the pages of my book and rereading the passages I would be performing tonight. Every so often I looked up, but couldn't find Savannah. If only I could have found my calm and greeted her outside like a normal person. *Hey Sav, what's cooking? What's chillin'?*

What's grillin'?

This was why I couldn't at the time—because all of my greetings were food references.

Soon enough, bodies pressed around me, the temperature of the room kicking up a few degrees.

"Hello there," a man said from the other side of the table.

I looked up to find a balding man with a bushy mustache, about thirty years older than me.

Between Savannah and my reading tonight, I was in no state to chat, so after I looked up quickly, I glanced back down at my book. "Hello."

"What are you reading?"

"Uhh…" It was too embarrassing to say *my book*, so I twisted around in my chair to scan the room for someone I knew. The woman who had invited me, Savannah, really anyone at this point. "Excuse me."

Without glancing at the man, I stood abruptly and left the table. *Wouldn't be able to go back there for the night.* As I made my way to the cash bar, the lights flickered, then went down.

Across the room, I thought I saw Sav in a flash of blue shimmer, but I couldn't be sure with the low light.

Sav. Why had I run again? From even a hello? She didn't deserve that. *I should go over there right now and—*

The microphone squawked and the first speaker started her speech, but I didn't hear a word. The voice muffled against the pounding of my heart in my ears at the thought of speaking with Sav again. If I didn't do it before I got on stage, I didn't know if I would ever do it. My pool of courage was shallow, and the podium would drain it dry.

I threaded through the tables as quietly as I could, stopping where people blocked the way. Uttering a quiet "excuse me" when they didn't see me. My path spit me out behind her, and I stopped to take her in.

It was *definitely* her. Though we'd only spent a short time together, I would know the curve of her body anywhere. The way she stood. The way she tilted her head when she was listening.

I wiped my palms on the ruched fabric at my hips and forced my feet forward, pretending I was on wheels and using momentum to propel myself toward her. My body was in full rebellion mode—sweating, trembling, constricting in all the wrong places, but I refused to let it win, even if it meant embarrassing sweat stains on the podium.

"Savannah," I said, but I timed it at the moment applause rose. Savannah craned her head around anyway, freezing mid-clap and dropping her hands when she saw me. She recovered before I did and rushed toward me, taking me by the shoulders.

"You're on," she said, her lips brushing the side of my face as she whispered in my ear.

I pulled away. My eyes jumped between hers. "Now?"

"Yes, right now. Go." She turned me toward the stage and gave me a little shove. I glanced back at her, but she was making a little *go* motion. The applause had been going on for quite some time, and it struck me suddenly it was for *me*. "You've got this, Pink," she shouted.

Her words strengthened me. My body was still

rebelling, though. I staggered to the makeshift stage, somehow made it to the podium, and held on for dear life.

I cleared my throat.

"My name is Casey Day, and I wrote the book *Hoping for Home*."

The lights were too bright and I couldn't see Savannah, but a pocket of applause and a whoop rose from near her area. The skin under my tattoo heated as if the heart on the outside of my chest was coming alive. Or burning under all the light and stares of the people.

As I spoke, my mind wandered. This was all because of Savannah. If I had never met her, I may have done something great, but it wouldn't have been quite this great, in this specific way. Even if we couldn't be together again, she had to know that. And what if she left because I'd ignored her? It was unlikely, but possible. I needed her to know now.

Gripping the edge of the podium, my stomach in full somersault mode, I ended the section I was reading at the close of the paragraph. Applause. Instead of introducing the next passage, I glanced in the direction of Savannah. "There's something else I have to say."

The place was so quiet you could hear a pin drop. This did not help calm me.

"I don't think I would be up in front of you today if it wasn't for a very special woman, who most of you know and probably love. Because… she's really hard not to love once you meet her. Not only is she caring and capable, but she's done more for these kids than just about anyone in this room. And that's say something." I was babbling. My arms shook. I felt like I was about to throw up the granola bar I ate before the show. *Finish it up, Casey.* "Please give a round of applause to Savannah Burns."

The crowd whooped and applauded again. Savannah stepped into the light.

She looked like a goddess in her blue draped dress, with her hair tumbling over her shoulders. More graceful than ever, she inclined her head in a thank you. Thank you. Thank you.

"I loved her once," I said, the microphone screeching as if it, too, was surprised by my sudden outburst. "And I messed it up."

Savannah's eyes fluttered as she turned to me. Our gazes locked again, the same way they had outside, but I was determined not to get stuck in my head this time. "Savannah. Will you give me another chance?"

Savannah lifted her chin, then she placed a hand over her heart.

I placed mine in the same place, over my heart.

All at once, the world collapsed and went black.

Chapter 27

SAVANNAH

She just disappeared from view.

One moment she was there, the next she was gone, as if a trap door had opened up beneath her. I rushed to the stage as fast as I could, reaching her before anyone else and she was already propped up on her elbows, blinking, bewildered.

I ran over, knelt, and took her head in my lap, supporting her. She looked pale as vanilla ice cream. "Have you eaten anything today?"

She rubbed her eyes with her palms. "A granola bar, I think."

"That's it?"

"What's wrong?" Bethany, the organizer of this event and my rock, was the first to reach us. "Are you okay, Casey?"

"I'm fine, I'm fine. It was just the heat of the lights," Casey said, trying to get up.

I held her shoulders down. "No, you stay. Bethany, can you please get us a glass of water and a straw?"

Bethany nodded and disappeared, telling the crowd to give us some space. I would have to send her flowers when this was over. Not for this alone, but for everything. She was the most capable person I'd ever worked with.

"While you're holding my shoulders, mind

giving them a quick rub?"

I glanced down to see a smirk and a little color coming into Casey's cheeks. "You're... you're... incorrigible."

"You and your big words."

"That's the only one I've got."

Casey's eyelids fluttered down, her lashes painting the tops of her cheekbones. "How long do you think you'll hold my head in your lap like this?"

I barked a laugh. "Not much longer if you don't stop fidgeting and driving me crazy."

"You love it."

"You want to test me?"

"Yes. I do." The smile dropped from her face and she fixed a stare into my eyes. I wasn't sure if the fluttering heartbeat in the tips of my fingers was mine or hers. It didn't matter.

Bethany arrived with the glass of water and some damp napkins. Casey lay back and quieted down while Bethany helped me tend to her. After a few minutes, she had the full color back in her cheeks and we moved her off the stage and into a more private area. After force-feeding her, Bethany left us alone with a single wink.

"I've got this covered," she said as she left.

Casey played with the hem of her dress. "Well, I feel like a total idiot."

"Why?"

"Uh, because I created a scene?"

"What? The telling everyone you loved me part or the passing out on stage?"

She dropped her face into her hands. "Oh, God, both? Don't you have a speech to give tonight?"

"I don't have anywhere else to be."

Casey bounced her knee, glancing at the curtained off makeshift room. "Can we... go outside? For some air?"

"Sure," I said, sliding out of the chair. I offered my arm to her and she slung hers through it. We made our way outside and down the steps, slowly, methodically, then we headed toward the Mall. It reminded me of our Sunday skate so many years before. It brought back all those feelings of potential, of falling, the blooming of love in my chest.

It took all my willpower to wait for her to speak first. She had already declared her love for me, but none of it seemed real. I had to make sure.

Once we had passed the museum and walked onto the Mall, she slid her arm away from mine and stepped back.

"I'm dying to get out of these heels," she said.

The words burst whatever bubble I'd been perched on top of. I laughed and kicked up one of my heels, pulling it off. "Why don't you, then?"

Casey tilted her head toward me as I took my other shoe off and dug my feet into the soft, dewy grass. Closing my eyes, I lifted my face to the sky and took in a long breath. *Give me the strength to accept...*

Fingers twined into mine. "Why did you do this?" she asked softly.

I opened my eyes and cocked my head. "Take off my shoes? Because it felt right."

"No," Casey blinked. "Why did you do all this? The bill. All of it."

"For you," I said. "For me, too. I wanted to bring

something important through from start to finish to see if I could do it without going crazy."

"Well?"

"It's not done yet," I said, shrugging. "But most of the work is. Whatever happens now, happens. It's kind of out of my hands."

"Wow."

"What?"

Casey's eyes moved over me, then landed on mine, squinting. "You're different."

"Yeah, I am," I said. Those two words from her— *you're different*—were everything. They were better than a declaration of love. It meant she was seeing me now, as I was, rather than the wreck I'd been toward the end of our relationship.

"I had to make a change. I'd sensed it before I met you, but then you put into contrast everything wrong with my life. You taught me how to *live*. All that, what you saw, you were right. It was because I was unhappy. Stressed. It was… I'm babbling… I just…" I saw her move out of the corner of my eye, but didn't register her movement until her lips were on mine. The heels in her hand dropped to the grass with a light thunk as she slung her arms over my shoulders.

Her lips were everything I remembered and more. She tasted sweet, left over from something she had eaten or drank at the gala, or maybe just her, but it didn't matter. I couldn't help myself. I picked her up and swung her around.

Casey broke away and let out a laugh, throwing her head back as we spun. Her laugh healed whatever was left broken inside of me. As I let her slide down my body, it heated for the first time in months. Years, maybe. A spark lit the flames of life that had been dormant for so long. I leaned over and kissed her again, sweetly.

"I wish I could undress you right here," I said, then immediately wanted to stuff the words back in my mouth. We'd barely *talked*, and I jumped right to removing clothes?

Casey looked around, the familiar devil in her eyes. "What's stopping you?"

Now I was the one to let out a laugh. "I don't want to be arrested. Not tonight."

"Where's your sense of fun? You don't want to have sex in a prison cell?"

"Not so much a dream of mine," I said around a laugh. "But seriously. Are we doing this? Is this… really happening? I'm not dreaming, am I?"

Casey swallowed, shaking her head. "You're not dreaming."

I pulled away, giving her a little space to answer my next questions. "Can you ever forgive me for what I did to you?"

"You didn't do it to me. You were having trouble and I wasn't strong enough to stay."

My eyes burned with tears. She was blaming herself? "No, you didn't do anything. You did the smart thing by leaving and I'm proud of you for it. I'm the one who destroyed everything good in my life."

Casey wiped her nose. "Sometimes that's exactly what we need."

I tucked some of her hair behind her ear. "How did I let you slip away?"

"Laziness?" she said.

Sassy girl. I let out a laugh at the absurdity of the comment. So we were already joking about it. I could go with that, for now. We would have plenty of time to talk about it later, now I knew there would be a later.

"I'm so happy right now," I said when I had recovered control of my mouth again. "I'm here. You're here. I couldn't ask for anything more."

I kissed her again, never sure I would be able to stop kissing her.

She pulled away. "Me either. I'm finally home."

My heart was full enough to expand out of my chest. I placed my palm against her tattoo. "Me, too."

Chapter 28

Epilogue

CASEY

The moment I'd put my seatbelt on in our car, Savannah had tied a silk scarf around my eyes. I'm not one to complain about silk scarves and their many uses, but it felt like we'd been in the car for hours, and my stomach burbled uneasily.

"If you're going to blindfold me, you could drive a little less like a maniac."

"I'm sorry. The roads are so curvy through here."

"Are you going to tell me where you're taking me?"

"If I did that, what would be the point of blindfolding you?"

"I don't know… some elaborate sex game?"

Savannah's warm hand settled on my thigh, and for a moment I was struck dumb. Two years had passed since we'd found each other again at the gala. Two years apart. Two years together. There was a certain symmetry to it, like the wings of a butterfly.

It had taken a little while to get to know Savannah again, to relearn the curves of her personality. To learn her challenges. To support her. But it was worth it. Every step was worth it. As I covered her hand with mine, I could feel her strength.

"Have I told you how much I fucking love you?"

She chuckled. "Wait 'til you see where we're going."

"Won't you just tell me?" I lifted my hand and tugged at my blindfold.

She swatted my hand away, jerking the car into a swerve in the process. "Keep it on, woman. Do you want to kill us both?"

"I'm not even the one driving. How would *I* kill us both?"

"With your impatience. We're almost there. Calm down."

I reached out, messing with the knobs of the radio and settling on a throwback. "She's so high," I sang. "High above me, she's so lovely. That's you, baby!"

"You're something else."

I turned up the volume on the radio, belting the song at the top of my lungs. As I sang, I rolled down the window. Fresh air assaulted my nose. Not city air. We were in the country. I continued to belt the song out the window.

"You're going to scare the locals."

"The local deer?"

"Did you peek?"

"No. The air smells like a pine tree."

The car came to a stop, sending my head into the side of the window. Before I could move, Savannah barked an order. "Stay there. And don't touch your blindfold."

"Aye aye, captain." I saluted to the sound of her closing her door. After about a second, I grew impatient and unbuckled myself, then opened my door.

"You," Savannah shouted, taking my arm.

"You adore me." I tried to wink, but the blindfold rendered it impossible.

She pulled me forward. After so long in the car, my feet were unsteady and I stumbled a little. Savannah held me with a firm grip. "You're right. I adore you."

"How much?" I glanced toward where her voice was coming from.

Savannah pinched me lightly. "Do we have to play this game right now?"

The air was crisp and heavy with pine. We were in the forest, somewhere. The ground was soft under my feet, the sun warming me intermittently. "Humor me. How much?"

"To the moon and the stars, of course."

"Is that it? Because I'm loving you out to the edges of the infinite universe."

"Do you always have to win?"

"I have to take my wins when I can get them with you around. Can I take this off now?"

"Only if you want to spoil the surprise."

"I don't care," I said, lifting my free arm. "I…"

I stopped dead. We stood in a grove of trees, a carpet of golden pine needles under our feet. Ahead, a log cabin stood in the middle of a clearing. "Are we on vacation or something? I thought you had a meeting tomorrow."

"I did. I do, but I couldn't wait any longer." Savannah bit the inside of her cheek, braiding her arms together and clasping her hands.

"Okay, so, why are we here? Are we breaking in?"

"It's yours," she said, her hands splitting and gesturing toward the house. "If you want it."

I blinked, testing my limbs to make sure everything still functioned properly. My brain certainly wasn't. "I don't understand."

"I bought you a house, Casey. It's yours."

"You…" I blinked. This time when I looked at the log cabin, a beam of sunlight fell on its moss-covered roof. I stepped toward it. *Mine?*

"Are you angry with me?"

"Angry? How could I be angry? This is the sweetest…" I pressed my hand to my chest as a sob swelled there. *Shit.* "Now look what you've done. You're making me cry."

Savannah caught my hand and pulled me into her body, wrapping her arms around me. "It was the least I could do after…"

"Stop it," I whispered into her hair. I placed a hand on the back of her neck. "You gave me a house and a law. You have nothing to be sorry for. Ever. Again."

"Can I get that in writing?" she said, pulling back.

With my eyes wide open I planted a kiss on her mouth. "How's that for writing?" I said, pulling away.

"Good enough." Savannah smiled, her fingers trailing her lips as if she could still feel our kiss. "Well, do you want to see it?"

"Of course." I threaded my arm back through Savannah's and tried to skip-drag her to the door. At the threshold, I stopped.

A house that was *mine? All mine?* I shook my head. We were in a dream. I must be dreaming this all up. The moss. The sunshine. The golden carpet. It was like a freakin' fairy tale. Savannah pulled a key from her bag and unlocked the door.

"You first," she said.

The door opened on a dusty, but cute entryway. Still standing outside, I peered in. I could see a room that would be a living room off to the left. The kitchen off to the right. "It needs some work," I said.

"I thought we could work on it together, on the weekends."

"That sounds amazing."

"Are you going in?"

I gave Savannah one last look before going inside. My beautiful, wonderful, smart, sassy, love of a woman. She'd given me a house. My throat clogged and my eyes swam with tears. I groaned, and leaned over, scooping her into my arms.

Savannah screamed, struggling, and I staggered under her weight. "Stop fighting," I said, laughing.

We made it through the door before falling to the ground in a laughing mess. I laughed so hard my chest hurt and the tears flowed. As I calmed, I made sure to capture this moment in my mind. I threaded my fingers through Savannah's and squeezed. She smiled back, her cheeks caving into those dimples. This. This was the happiest moment of my life. Savannah had given me a house, sure, but she'd also given me a home.

We'd been through so much and come out the other side closer than ever. Together we would build both house and home to last a lifetime.

Join my mailing list for a bonus chapter of Sav & Casey building their house and home.

Author's Letter

Hello, love—

Typically, this is where I tell you how much a review on Amazon and Goodreads means to authors like me and ask you to join my mailing list for the thousandth time. But if you've read this far, you deserve a letter.

(I like writing letters. Real letters. In fact, if you write me a letter, I'll write one back. Address: Anna Cove, PO Box 104, Rexford, NY 12148).

You, dear reader, since you've spent so much time with my words, you deserve… drum roll… MORE WORDS. Some non-fictional ones. Though the fictional words often have a scarier, deeper truth to them than the "true" ones.

Here's my best attempt at true truth:

While I wrote this book, I was reading *I'll Be Gone in the Dark* by Michelle McNamara. Michelle was Patton Oswalt's wife and a brilliant writer of true crime, among (many) other things. Notice the "was." Michelle passed away at the age of 46 in 2016 due to a mix of drugs in her system and heart problems. Knowing this, almost as soon as I picked up the book and started reading her beautiful words, my heart screamed. *It's not fair. Why? WHY?*

Last week, as I was editing *Halfway Home*,

I put down my stack of marked up pages and started googling. I couldn't help it. Michelle had wormed her way into my mind. I wasn't so much obsessed with her obsession—the Golden State Killer—as I was with *her*. Her words had made me fall in love with her. The fact she was gone haunted me. (It didn't pass over my head that she had died, in part, because of the drugs I was writing about.) I stumbled on the obituary her husband wrote for *Time* and, unfortunately scrolled down to the comments.

What I found horrified me. I should have known. Comment sections are often cesspool-like in nature, but I looked, thinking I would find the love and heartbreak I was feeling. What I found instead were posts blaming her for her death as if she deserved it and posts ridiculing Patton for his words. Then posts calling those commentators names.

I'm an optimist. I believe in people. Whenever someone says "people suck" I have this gut reaction. *No. No they don't. They do good things, too. Those things are just not interesting enough to dominate the news.* But the comments on the obituary made me live in that negative space for a moment. How could the commentators have such a disconnect with empathy? With love? How could they not imagine what losing a loved one feels like? Haven't we all lost someone important?

This is part of the problem of our time. Part of the question we have to solve. How can we use this vast, wonderful resource (the internet) to *connect* rather than take down? To empathize? To understand?

I swear this relates to *Halfway Home*.

The center of this book is forgiveness and empathy and connection. It's about second chances. It's about the destruction and rebuilding of trust. I was terrified writing it. Hell, I'm *still* terrified to put it out there. It's not as light as my other books. It deals with addiction and life satisfaction. Is it perfect? Absolutely not. But I'm more confident than ever about putting it out after reading the comments of Michelle's obit. I think we need stories about this right now. Because forgiveness is *hard*. Empathy is *hard*. We don't always think people deserve it. Sometimes, they don't right away.

I'm not expecting to change minds with this book. I just hope, in a small way, it reminds us how much we need to forgive others and feel for them, while also taking care of ourselves. It certainly did for me while writing. At one point, Casey says, "Hurt people hurt people." I believe this is true. So take care of yourself, love. Find what you need to heal. Find your joy. Fill your cup, then share it with others.

Okay, I'm getting preachy which is a sign for me to hit "publish" on this thing.

As always, thank you for reading! It means the world to me.

Love,
Anna

Find me Online

Website & blog: **annacove.com**.
Twitter: **@AnnaCoveAuthor**.
Facebook: **facebook.com/annacoveauthor**

31507999R00138

Printed in Great Britain
by Amazon